DERIB + JOB

YAKARI
IN THE LAND OF WOLVES

9th CINEBOOK
The 9th Art Publisher

Original title: "Yakari au Pays des Loups"

Original edition: © LE LOMBARD (Dargaud-Lombard s.a.) 1981, by DERIB + JOB
www.lelombard.com

English translation: © 2008 Cinebook Ltd

Translator: Erica Jeffrey
Lettering and text layout: Imadjinn sarl
Printed in Spain by Just Colour Graphic

This edition first published in Great Britain in 2008 by
CINEBOOK Ltd
56 Beech Avenue
Canterbury, Kent
CT4 7TA
www.cinebook.com

A CIP catalogue record for this book
is available from the British Library

ISBN: 978-1-905460-29-8

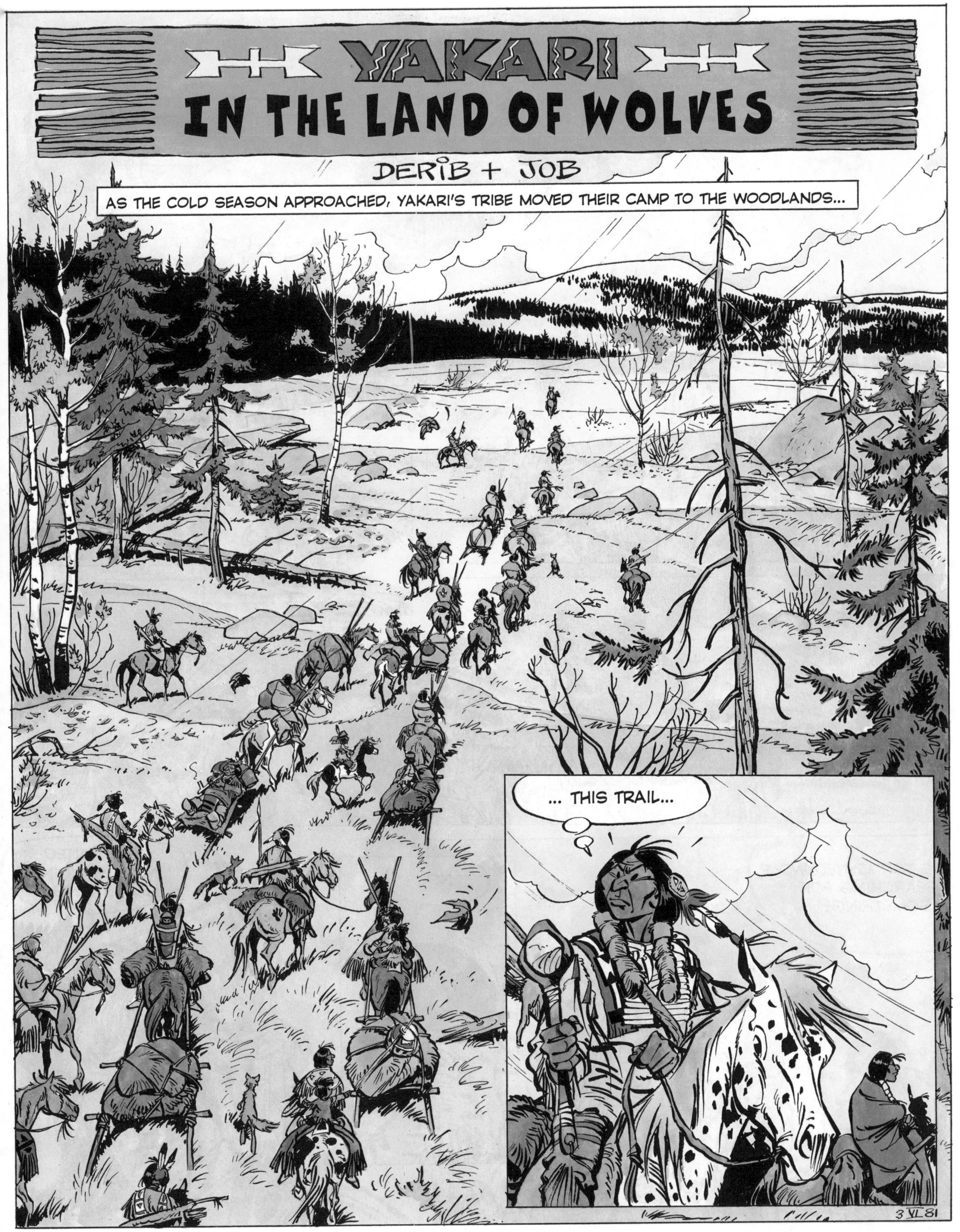
YAKARI
IN THE LAND OF WOLVES
DERIB + JOB
AS THE COLD SEASON APPROACHED, YAKARI'S TRIBE MOVED THEIR CAMP TO THE WOODLANDS...
... THIS TRAIL...
3 VI 81

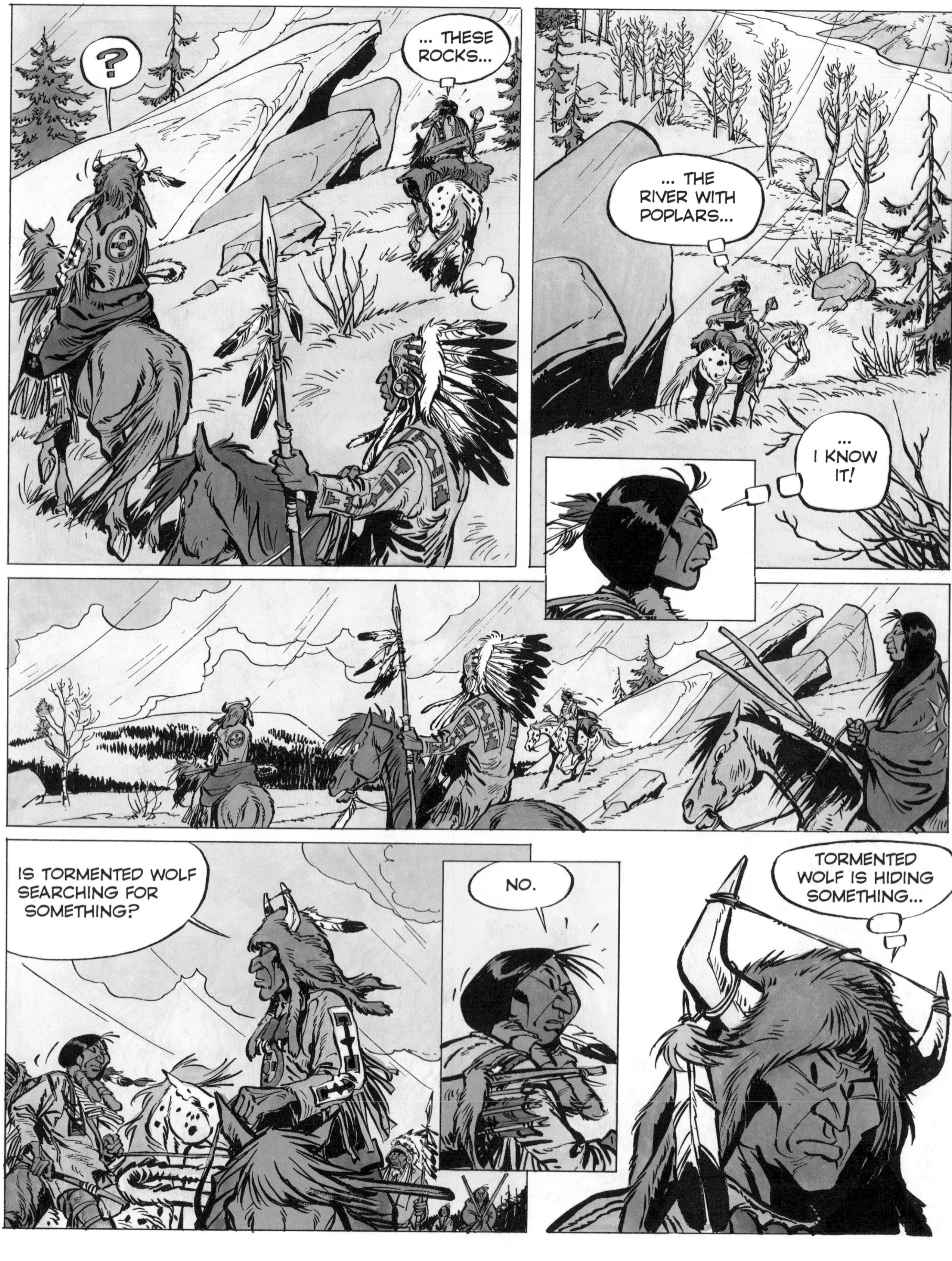
?
... THESE ROCKS...
... THE RIVER WITH POPLARS...
... I KNOW IT!
IS TORMENTED WOLF SEARCHING FOR SOMETHING?
NO.
TORMENTED WOLF IS HIDING SOMETHING...

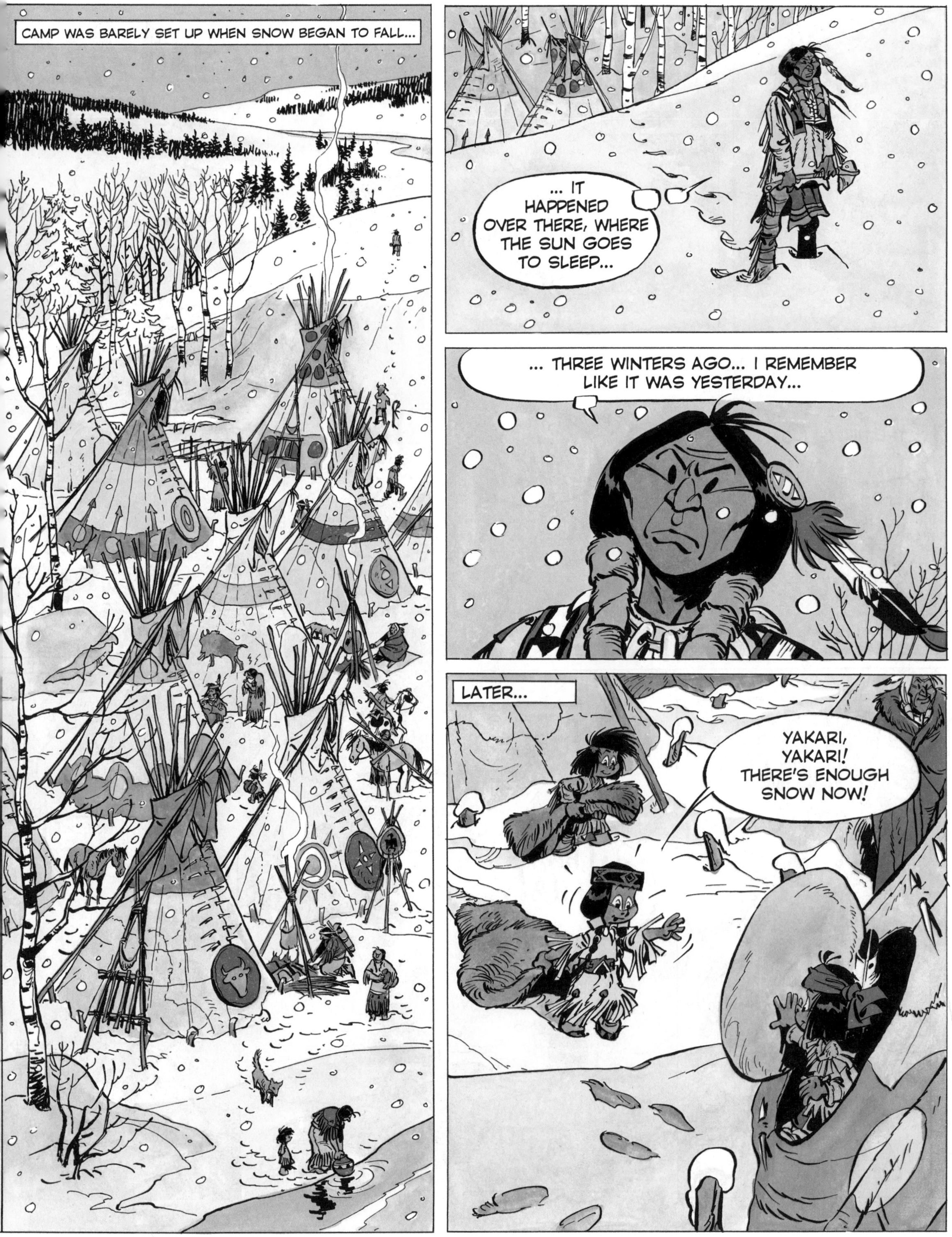
CAMP WAS BARELY SET UP WHEN SNOW BEGAN TO FALL...
... IT HAPPENED OVER THERE, WHERE THE SUN GOES TO SLEEP...
... THREE WINTERS AGO... I REMEMBER LIKE IT WAS YESTERDAY...
LATER...
YAKARI, YAKARI! THERE'S ENOUGH SNOW NOW!

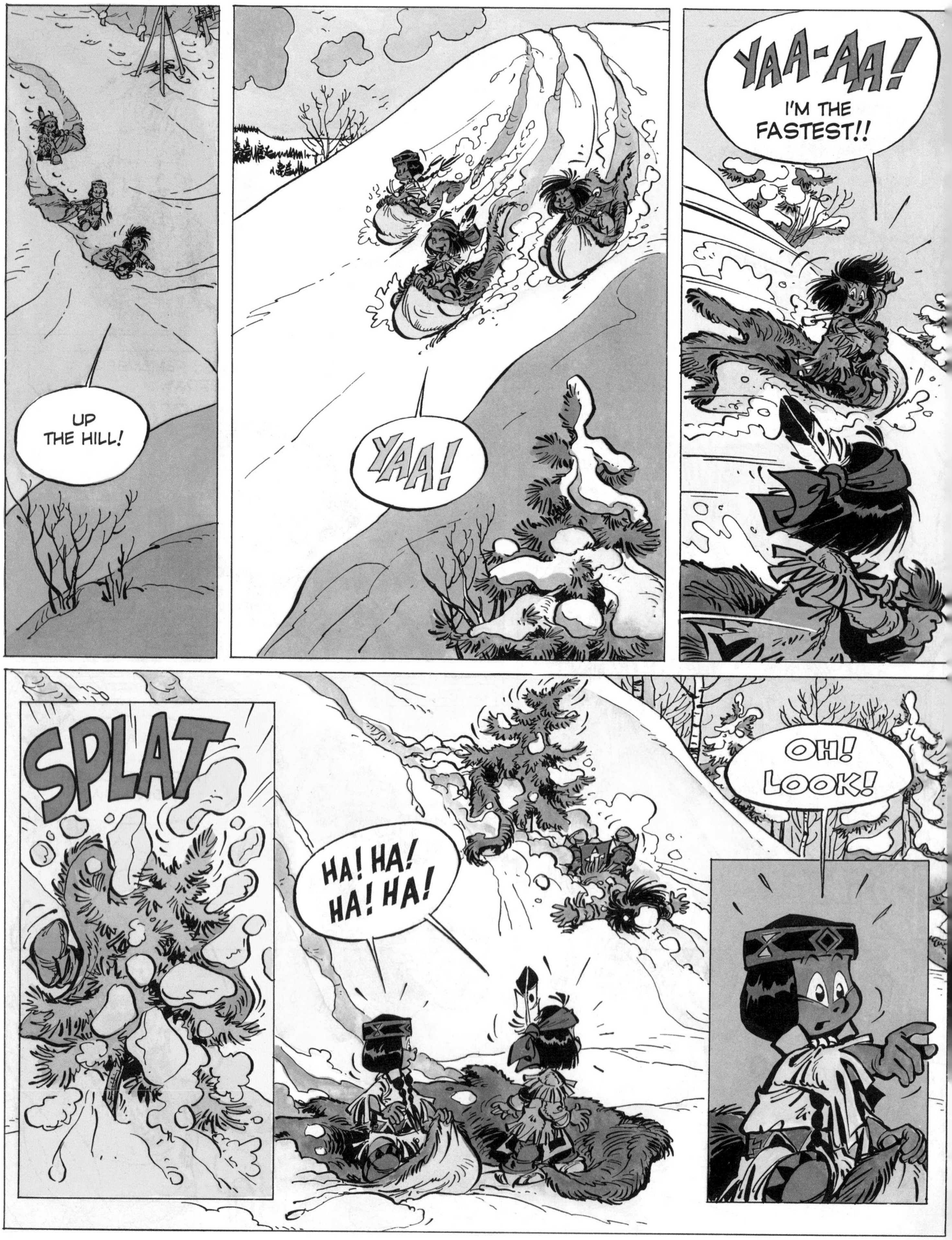

UP THE HILL!
YAA!
YAA-AA! I'M THE FASTEST!!
SPLAT
HA! HA! HA! HA!
OH! LOOK!

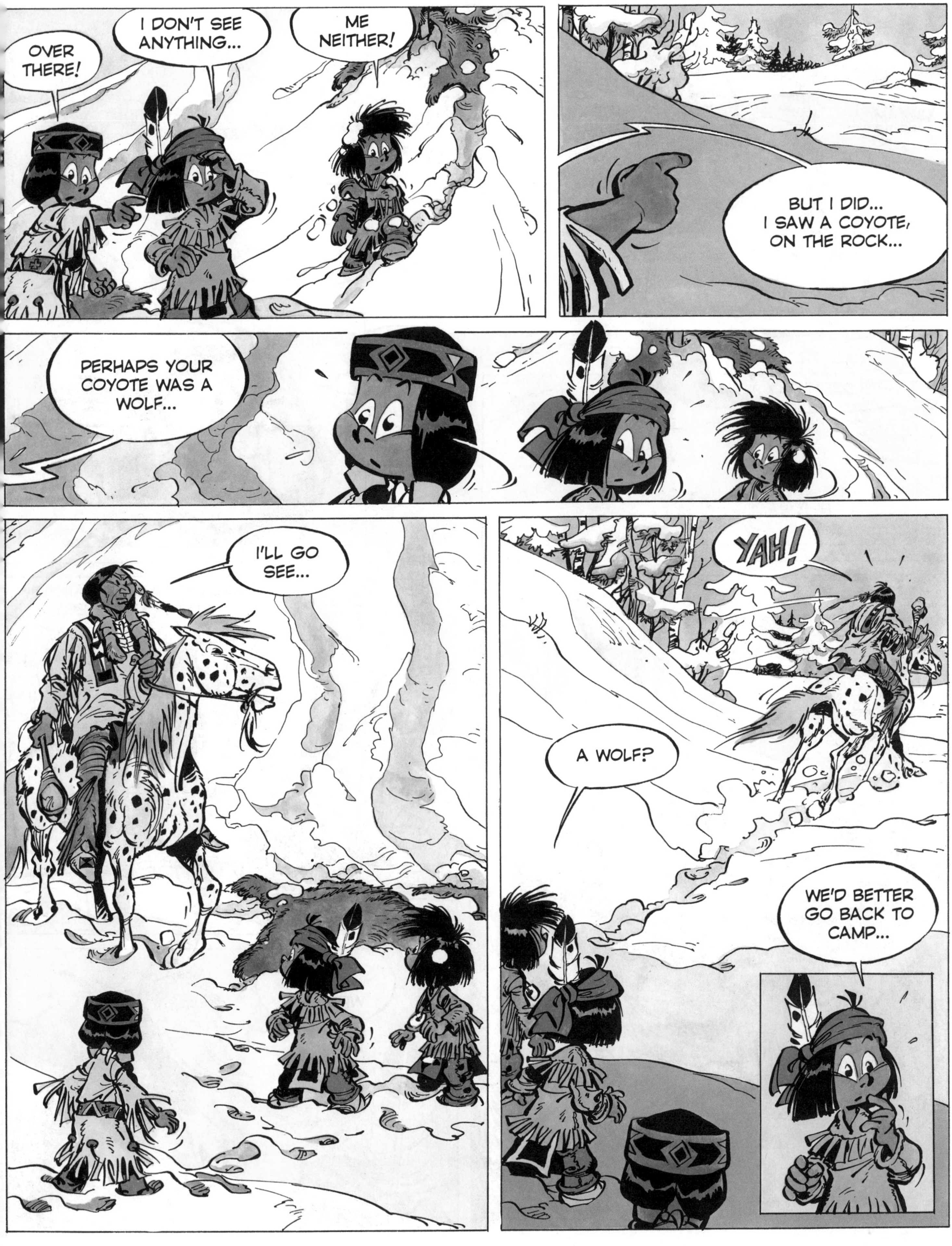
OVER THERE!
I DON'T SEE ANYTHING...
ME NEITHER!
BUT I DID... I SAW A COYOTE, ON THE ROCK...
PERHAPS YOUR COYOTE WAS A WOLF...
I'LL GO SEE...
YAH!
A WOLF?
WE'D BETTER GO BACK TO CAMP...

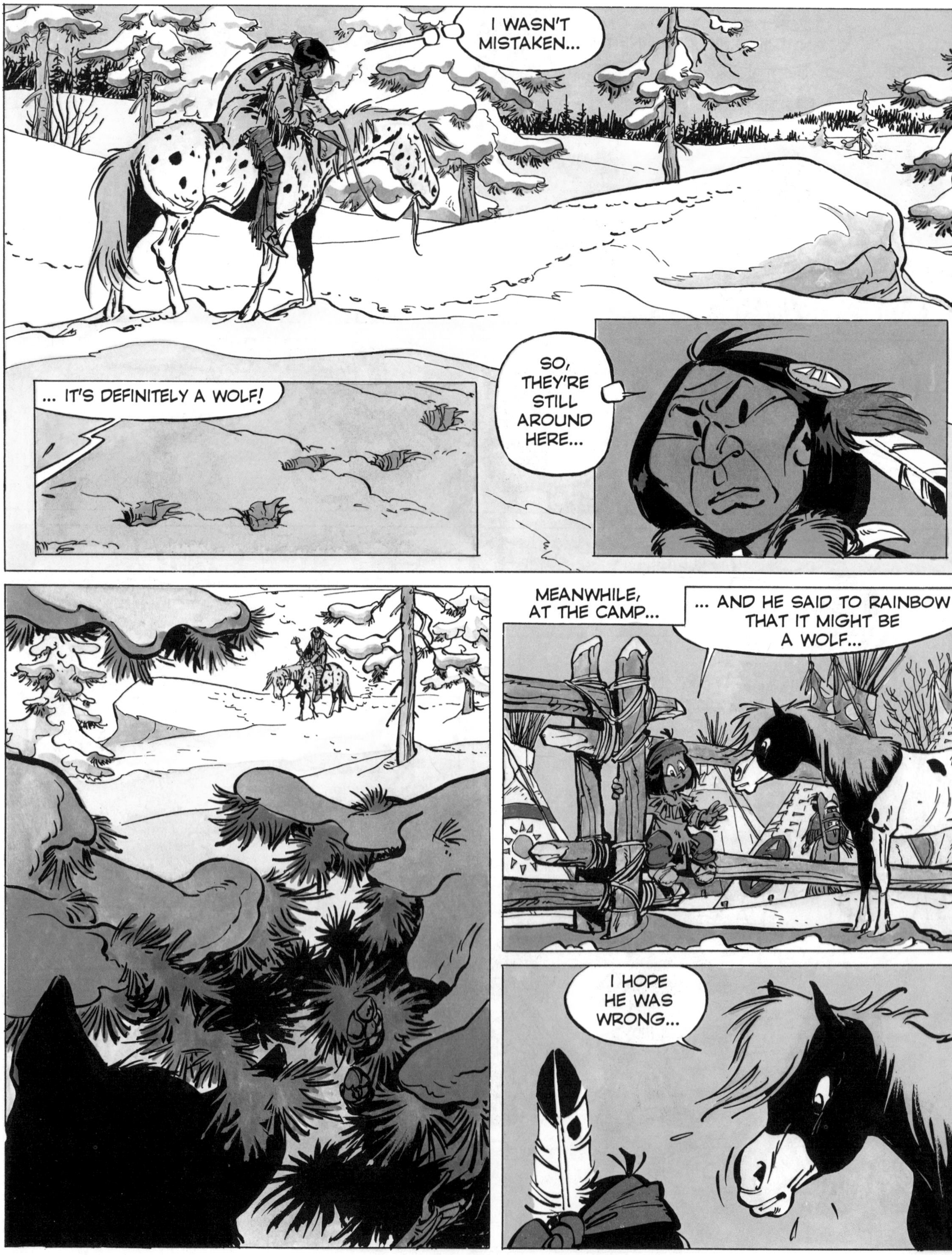
I WASN'T MISTAKEN...
... IT'S DEFINITELY A WOLF!
SO, THEY'RE STILL AROUND HERE...
MEANWHILE, AT THE CAMP...
... AND HE SAID TO RAINBOW THAT IT MIGHT BE A WOLF...
I HOPE HE WAS WRONG...

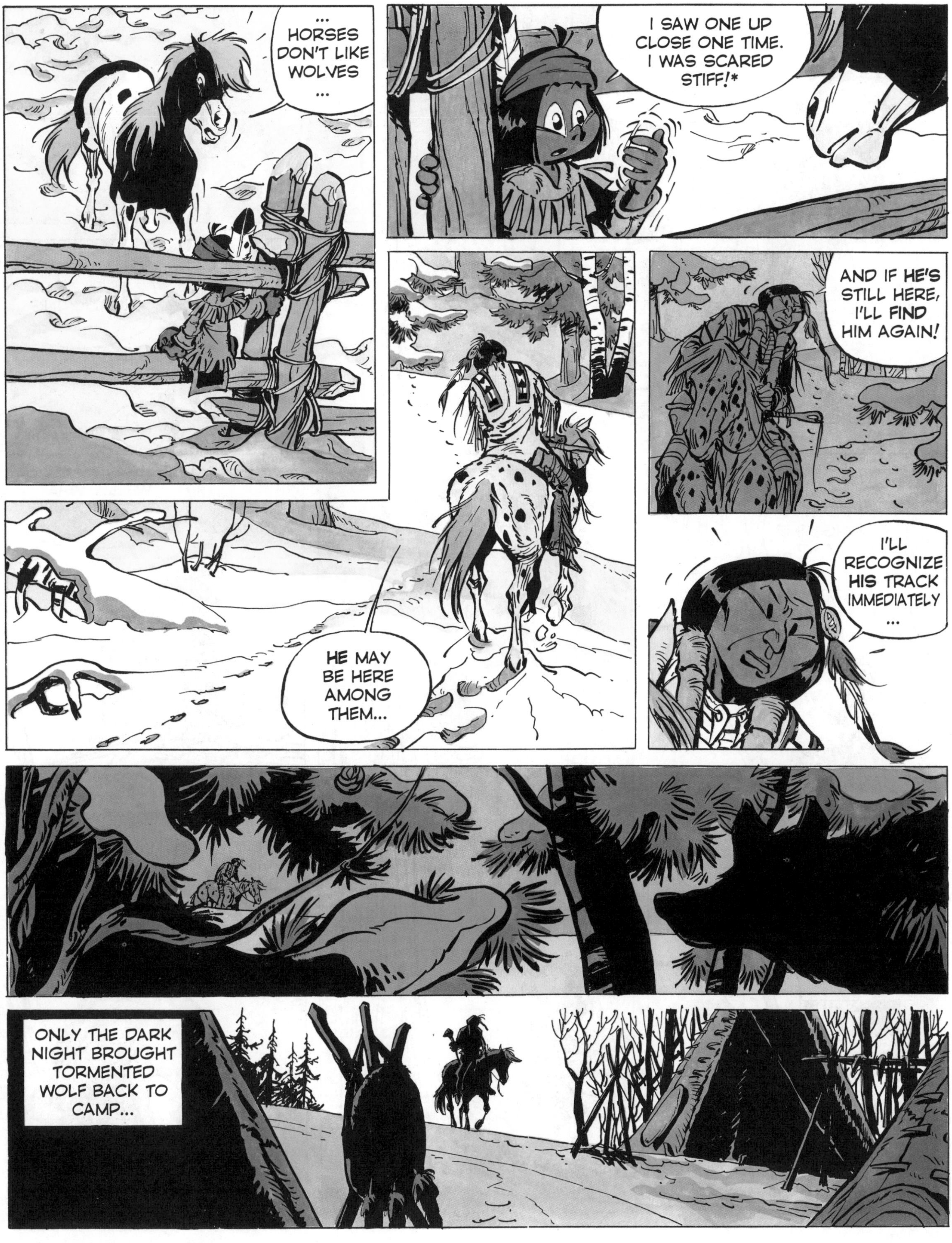
... HORSES DON'T LIKE WOLVES ...
I SAW ONE UP CLOSE ONE TIME. I WAS SCARED STIFF!*
AND IF HE'S STILL HERE, I'LL FIND HIM AGAIN!
HE MAY BE HERE AMONG THEM...
I'LL RECOGNIZE HIS TRACK IMMEDIATELY ...
ONLY THE DARK NIGHT BROUGHT TORMENTED WOLF BACK TO CAMP...

* SEE *YAKARI AND GREAT EAGLE*

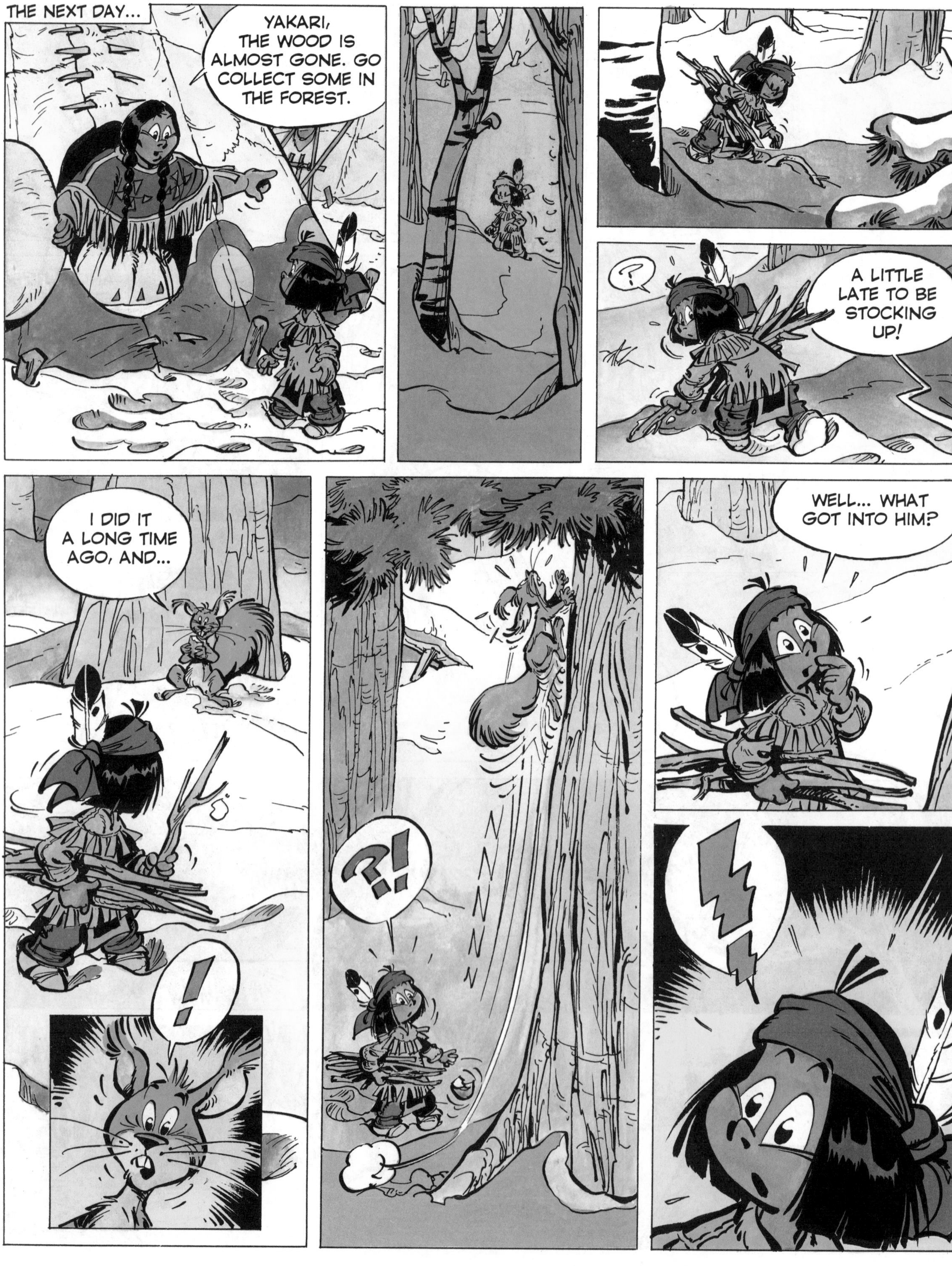
THE NEXT DAY...
YAKARI, THE WOOD IS ALMOST GONE. GO COLLECT SOME IN THE FOREST.
?
A LITTLE LATE TO BE STOCKING UP!
I DID IT A LONG TIME AGO, AND...
!
?!
WELL... WHAT GOT INTO HIM?

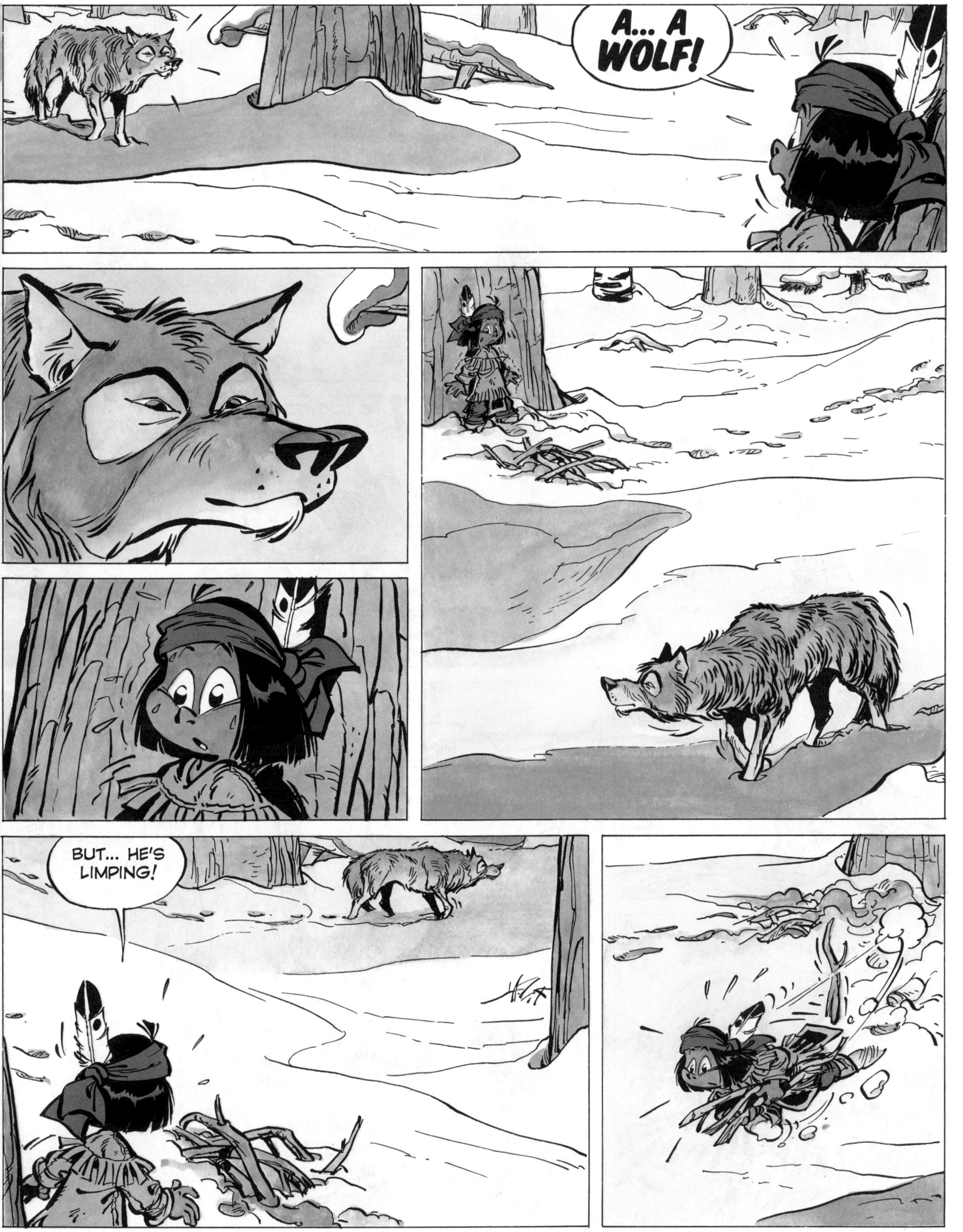
A... A WOLF!
BUT... HE'S LIMPING!

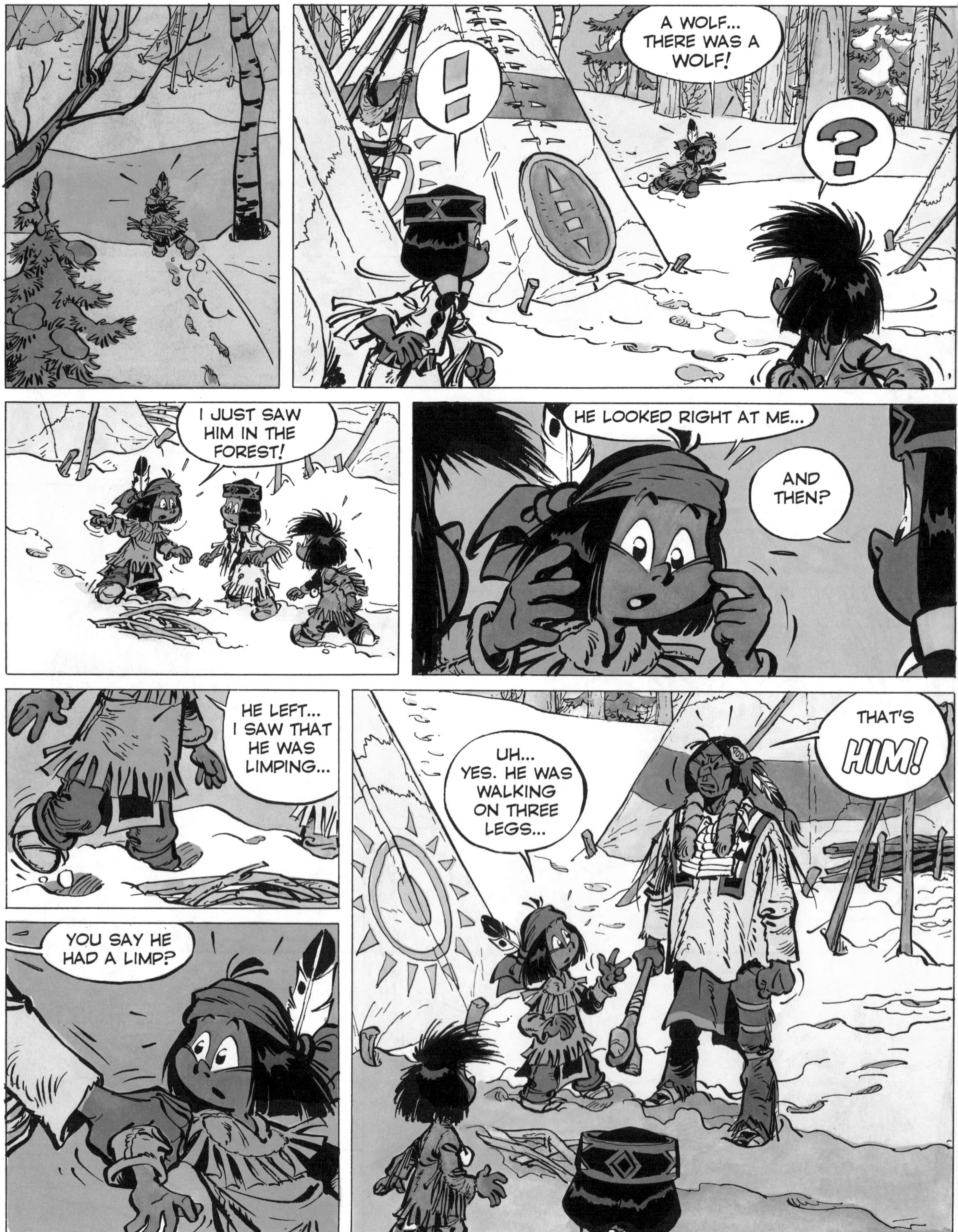
!
A WOLF... THERE WAS A WOLF!
?
I JUST SAW HIM IN THE FOREST!
HE LOOKED RIGHT AT ME...
AND THEN?
HE LEFT... I SAW THAT HE WAS LIMPING...
YOU SAY HE HAD A LIMP?
UH... YES. HE WAS WALKING ON THREE LEGS...
THAT'S HIM!

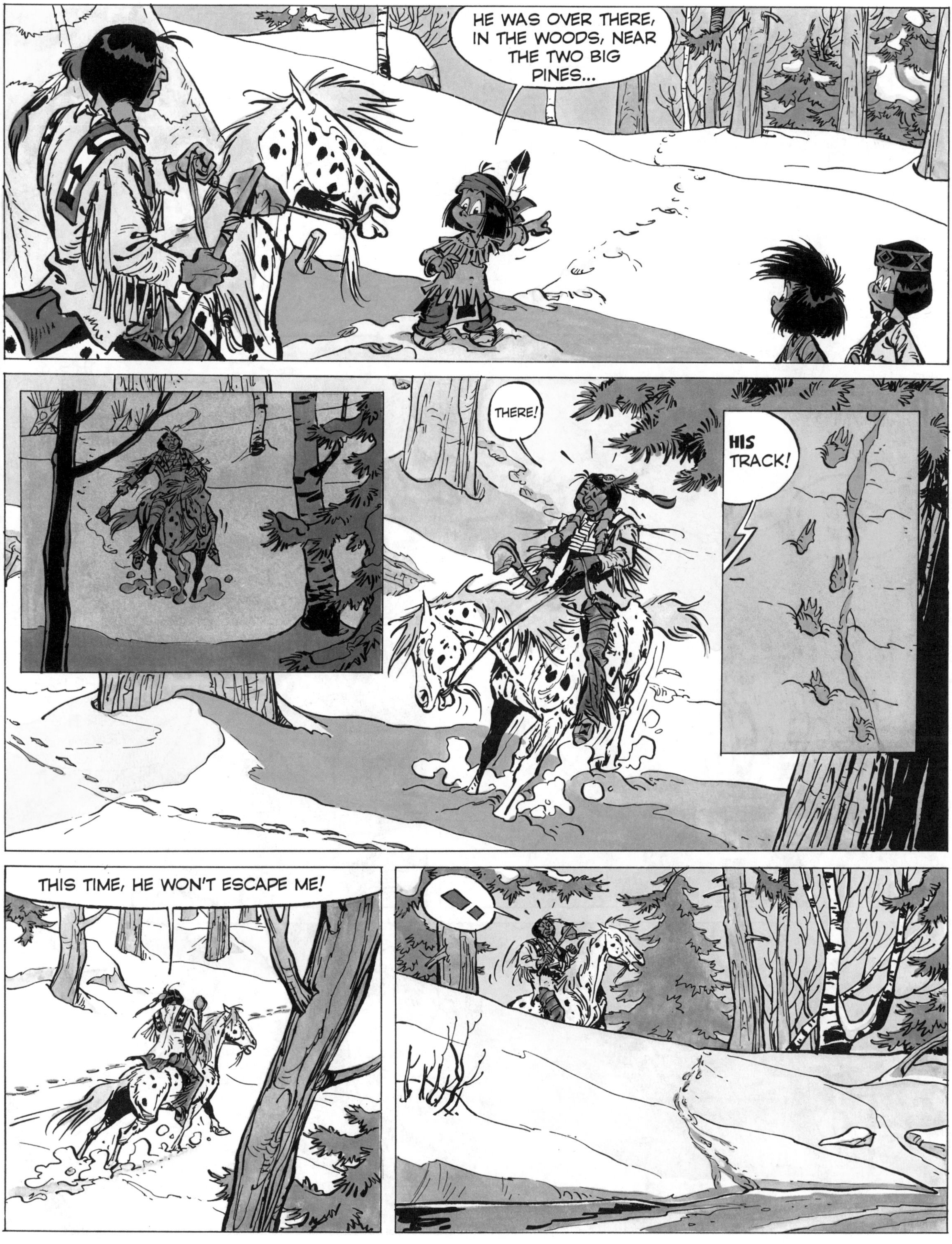
HE WAS OVER THERE, IN THE WOODS, NEAR THE TWO BIG PINES...
THERE!
HIS TRACK!
THIS TIME, HE WON'T ESCAPE ME!

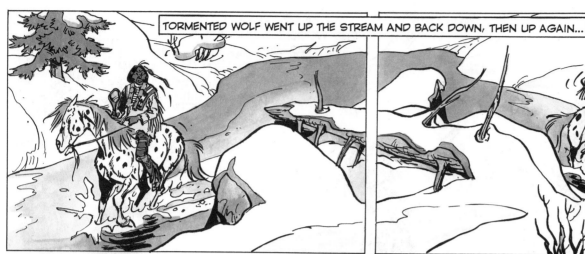

TORMENTED WOLF WENT UP THE STREAM AND BACK DOWN, THEN UP AGAIN...

?!

THIS IS WHERE THEY COME TO DRINK... HE'S CUNNING...

... HE KNOWS WHERE HE HAS TO CROSS TO COVER HIS TRACK!

HE MUST SENSE THAT I'M FOLLOWING HIM...

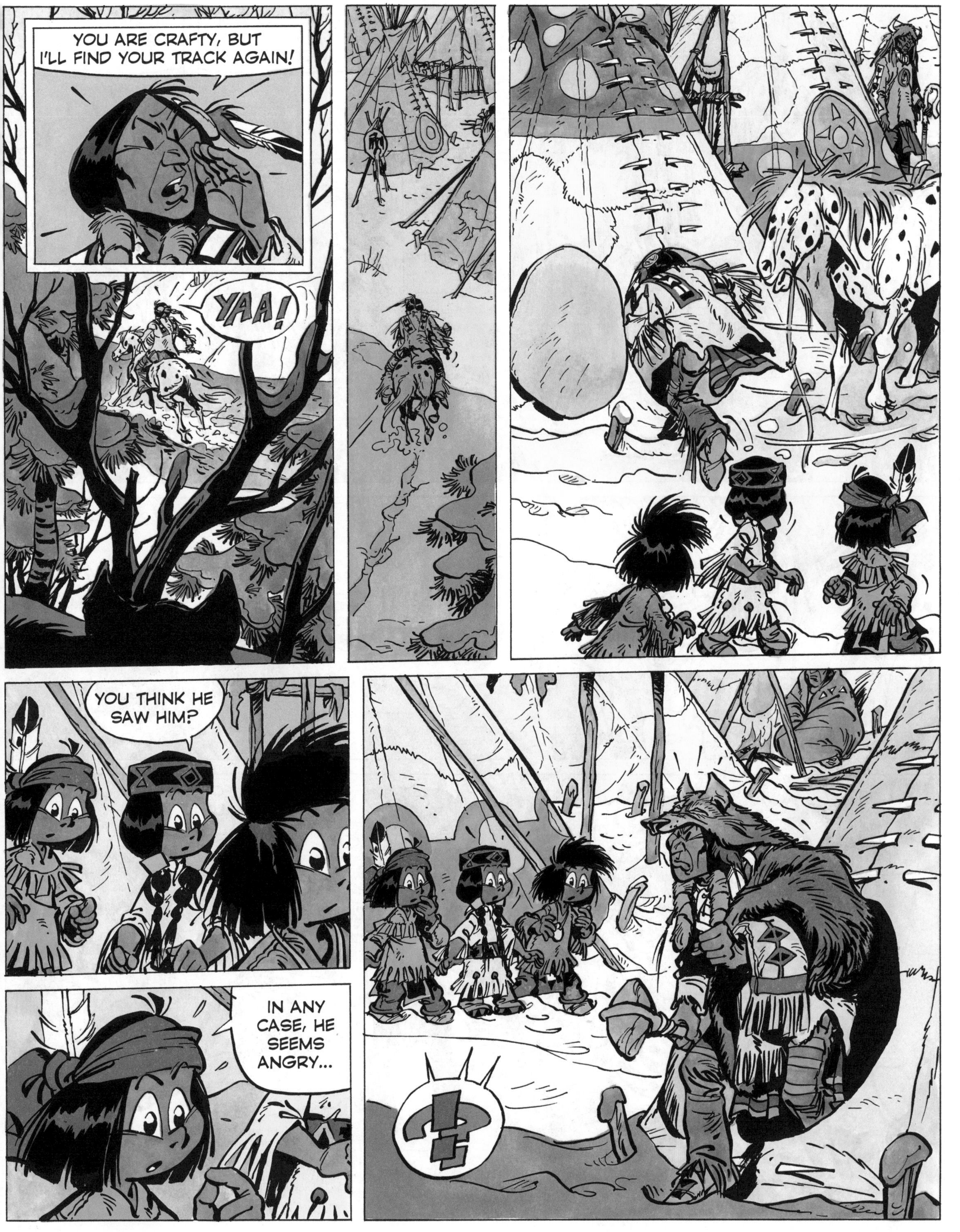
YOU ARE CRAFTY, BUT I'LL FIND YOUR TRACK AGAIN!
YAA!
YOU THINK HE SAW HIM?
IN ANY CASE, HE SEEMS ANGRY...
!?

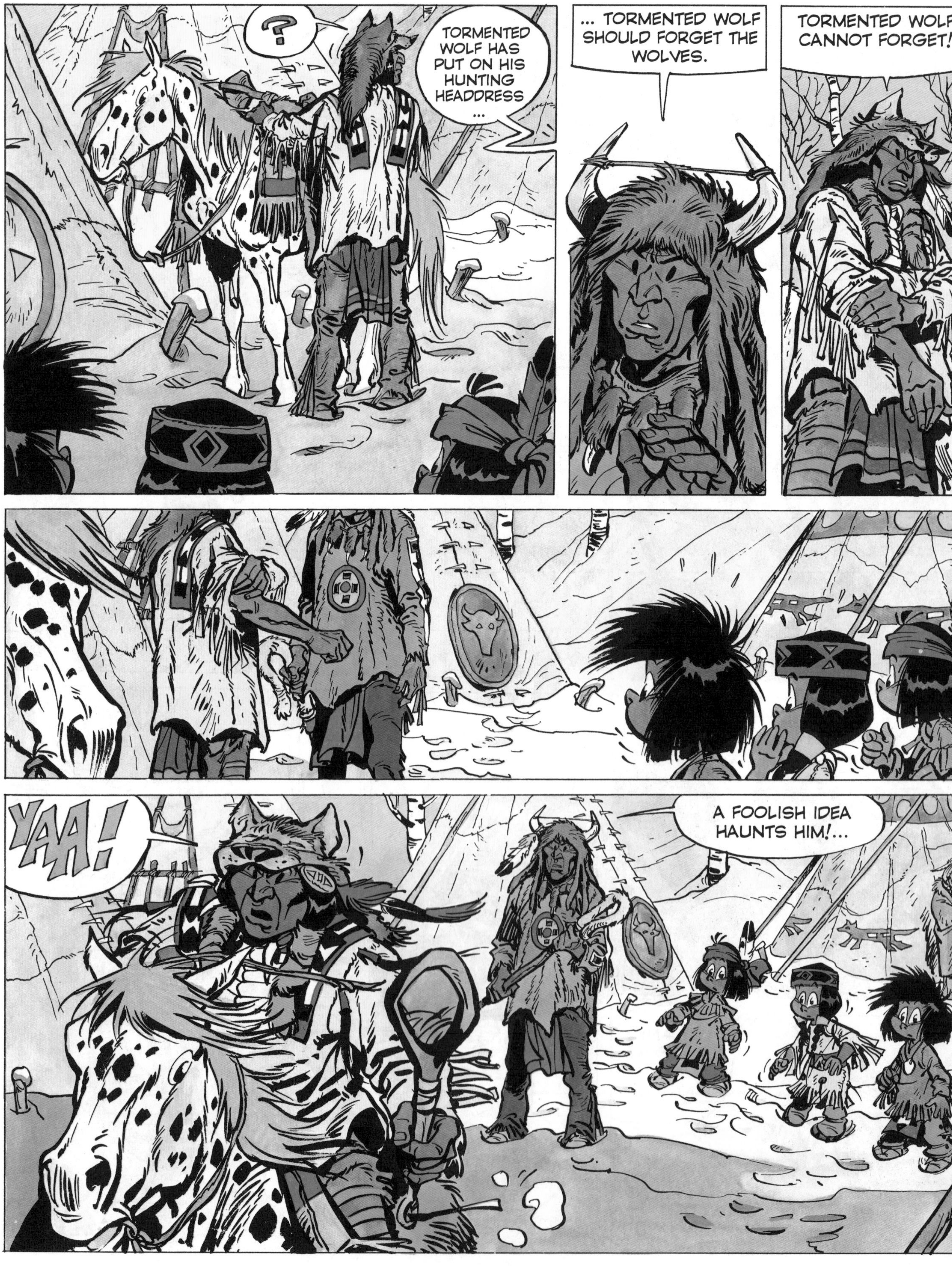
?
TORMENTED WOLF HAS PUT ON HIS HUNTING HEADDRESS ...
... TORMENTED WOLF SHOULD FORGET THE WOLVES.
TORMENTED WOLF CANNOT FORGET!
YAA!
A FOOLISH IDEA HAUNTS HIM!...

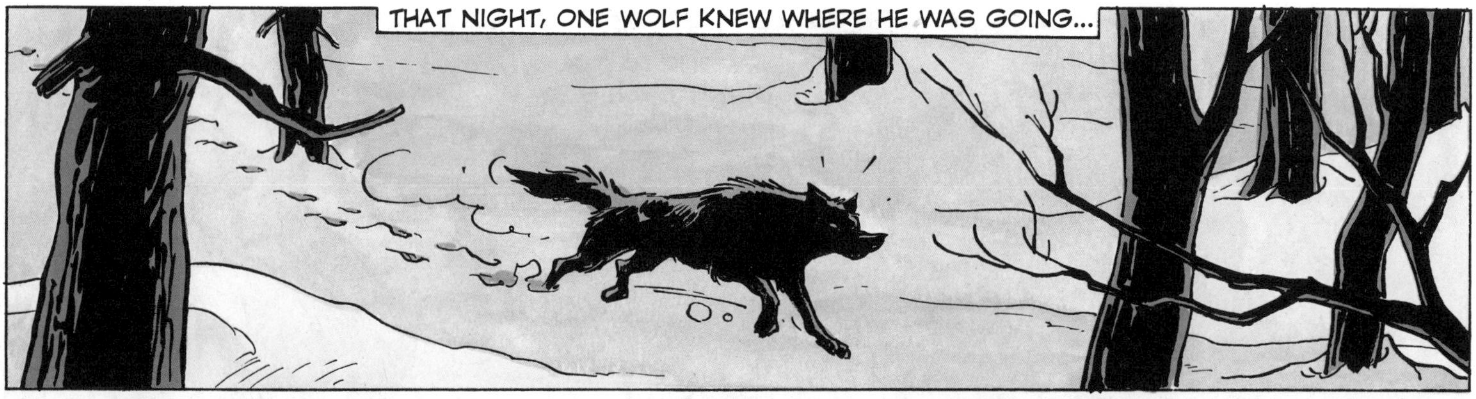
THAT NIGHT, ONE WOLF KNEW WHERE HE WAS GOING...

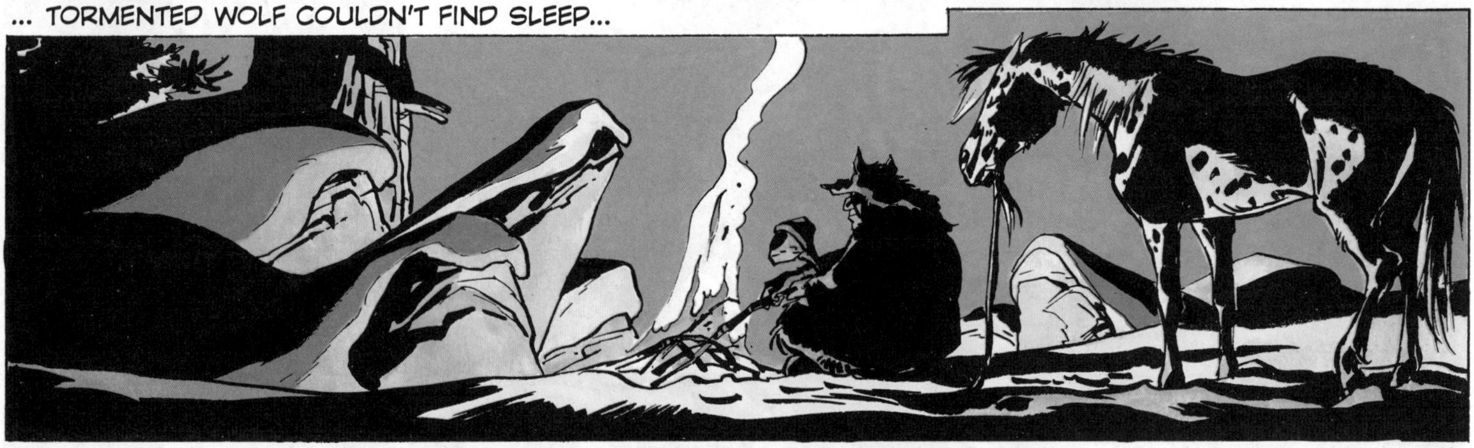
... TORMENTED WOLF COULDN'T FIND SLEEP...

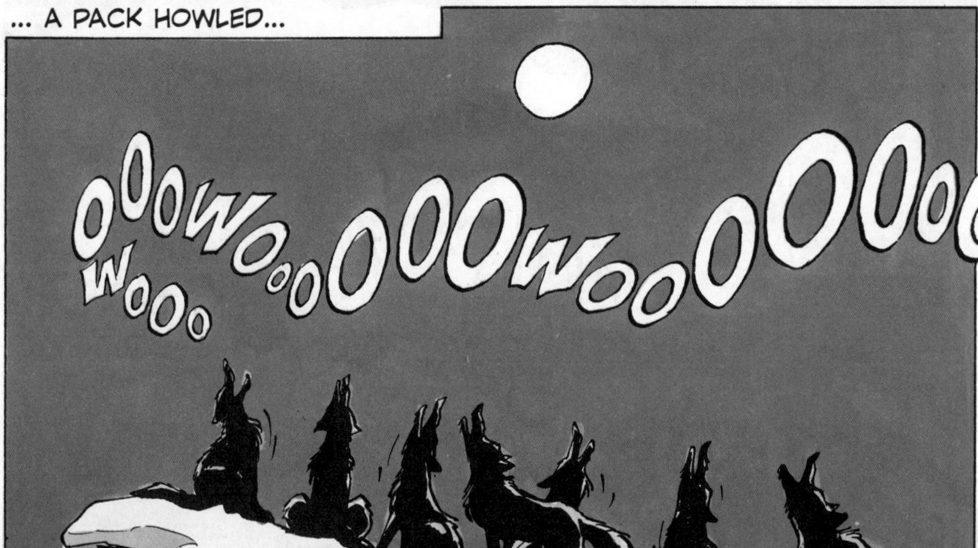
... A PACK HOWLED...
OOOWOOOOOOWOOOOOOOOOWOOOOOOO
WOOO

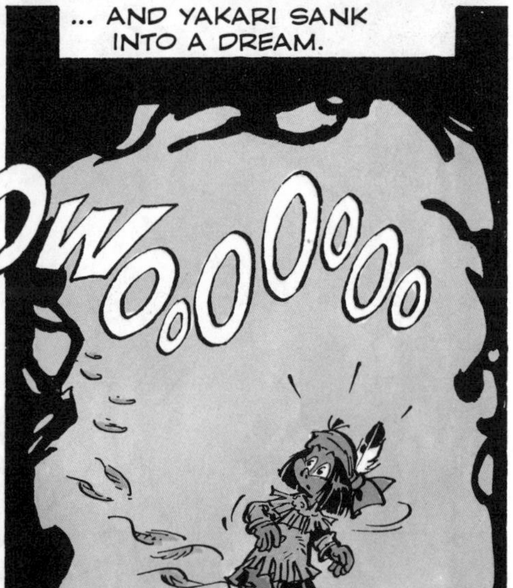
... AND YAKARI SANK INTO A DREAM.

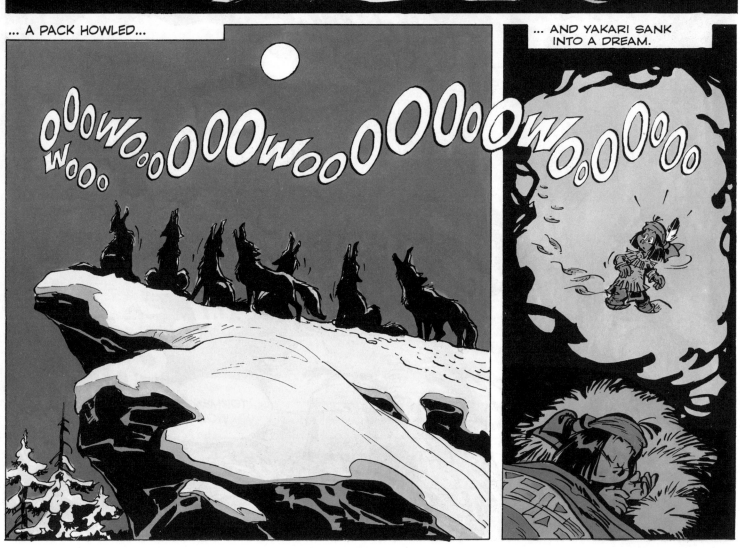

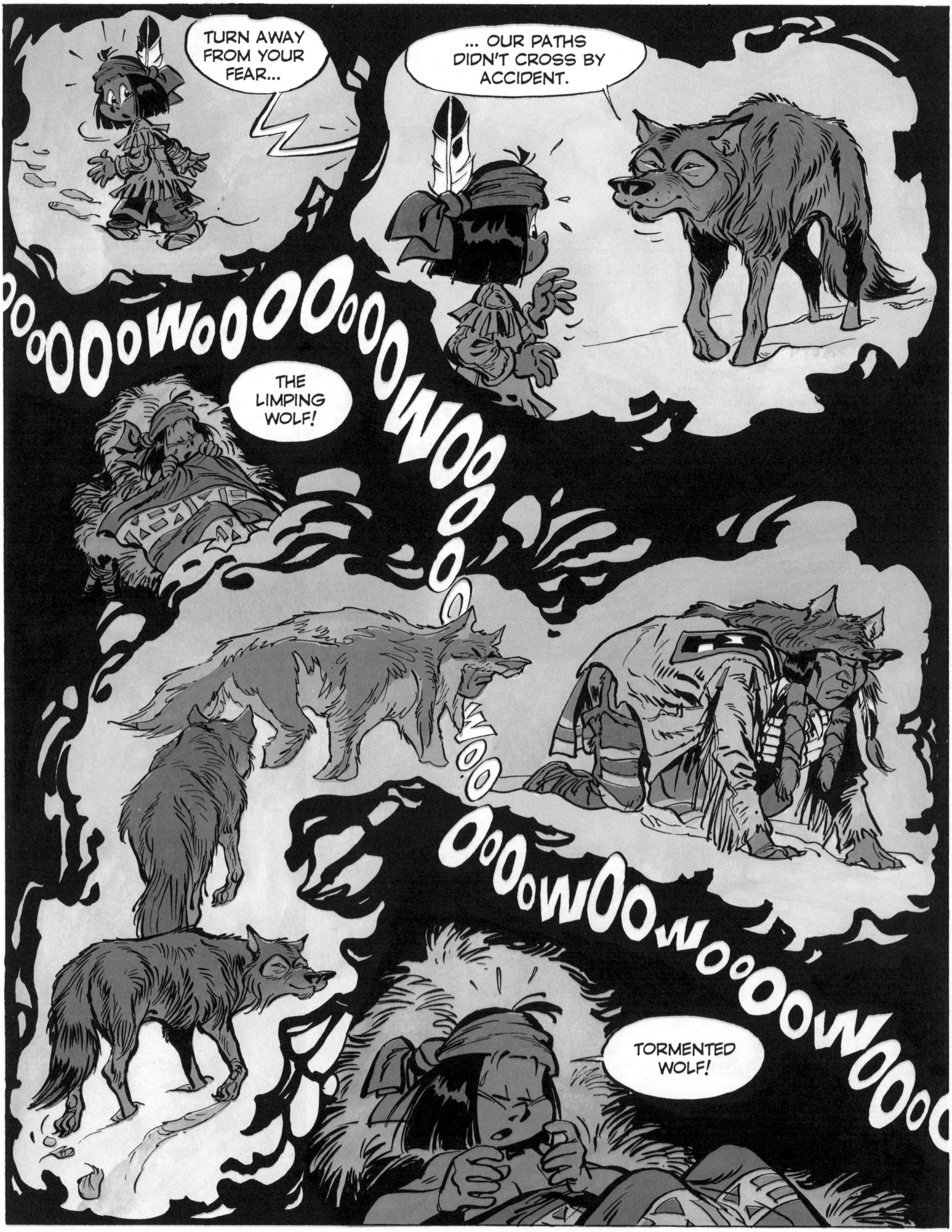
TURN AWAY FROM YOUR FEAR...
... OUR PATHS DIDN'T CROSS BY ACCIDENT.
OOOOOWOOOOOOOOWOOOOOOOO
THE LIMPING WOLF!
WOOOO
OOOOWOOWOOOOOOWOOOOO
TORMENTED WOLF!

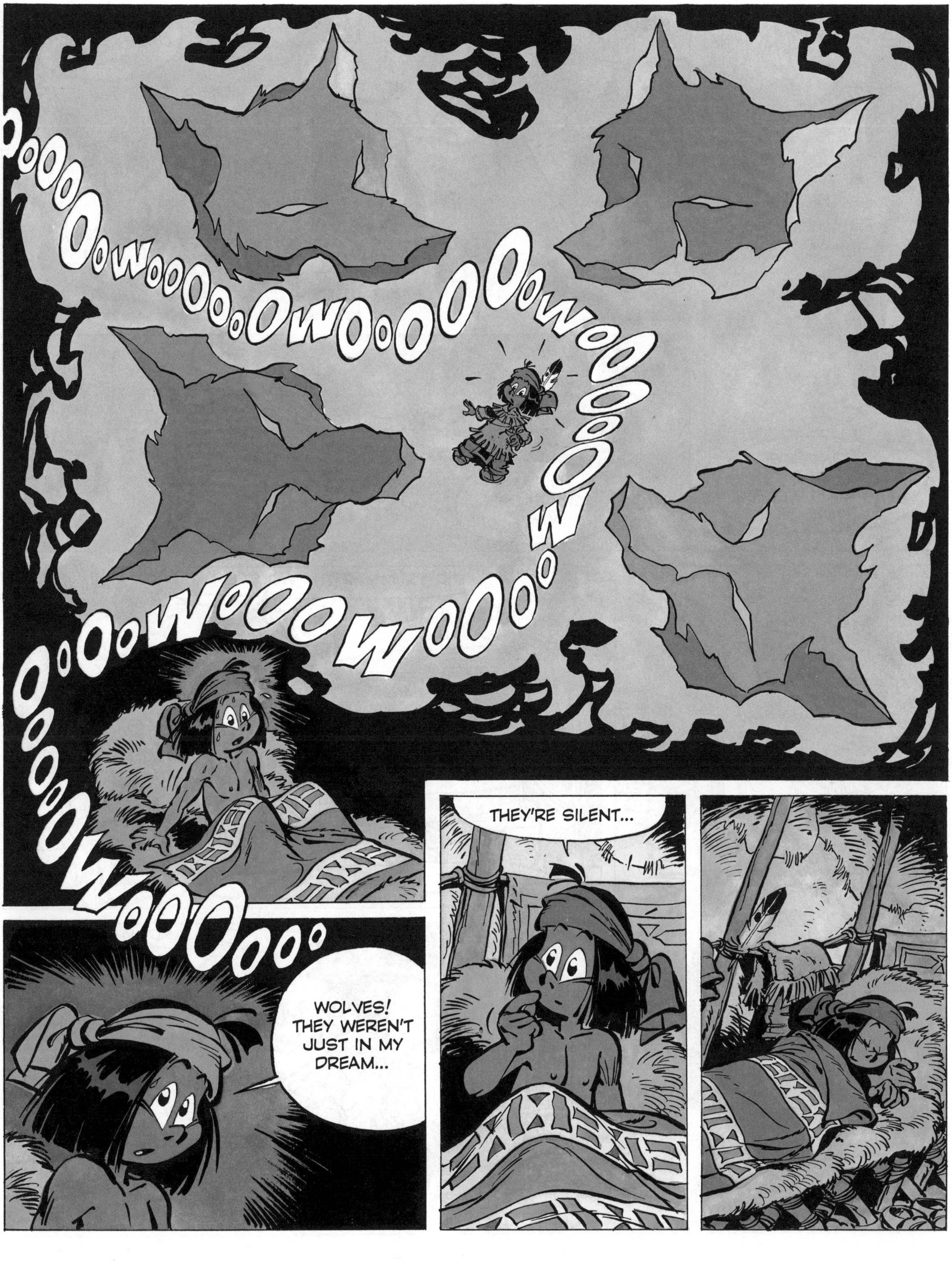
WOLVES! THEY WEREN'T JUST IN MY DREAM...
THEY'RE SILENT...

IN THE MORNING...

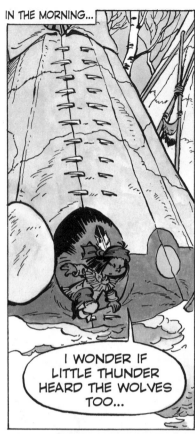

I WONDER IF LITTLE THUNDER HEARD THE WOLVES TOO...

I NEED TO FIND HIM!

THE LIMPING WOLF'S TRACKS!

HE CAME VERY CLOSE... WHY?

DID YOU HEAR THE WOLVES?

AND WHAT'S MORE, I DREAMED ABOUT THEM!

20

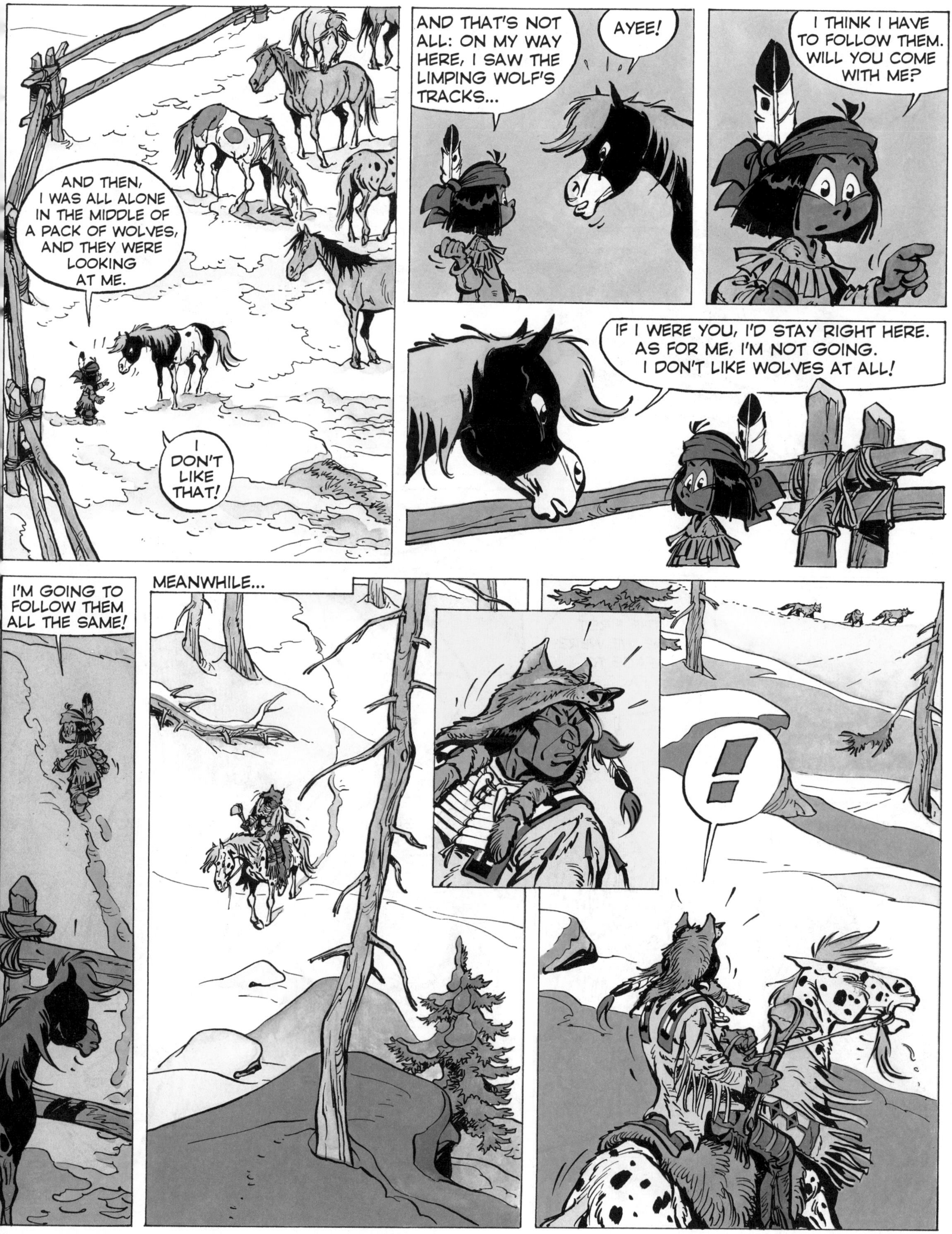

AND THEN, I WAS ALL ALONE IN THE MIDDLE OF A PACK OF WOLVES, AND THEY WERE LOOKING AT ME.
I DON'T LIKE THAT!
AND THAT'S NOT ALL: ON MY WAY HERE, I SAW THE LIMPING WOLF'S TRACKS...
AYEE!
I THINK I HAVE TO FOLLOW THEM. WILL YOU COME WITH ME?
IF I WERE YOU, I'D STAY RIGHT HERE. AS FOR ME, I'M NOT GOING. I DON'T LIKE WOLVES AT ALL!
I'M GOING TO FOLLOW THEM ALL THE SAME!
MEANWHILE...
!

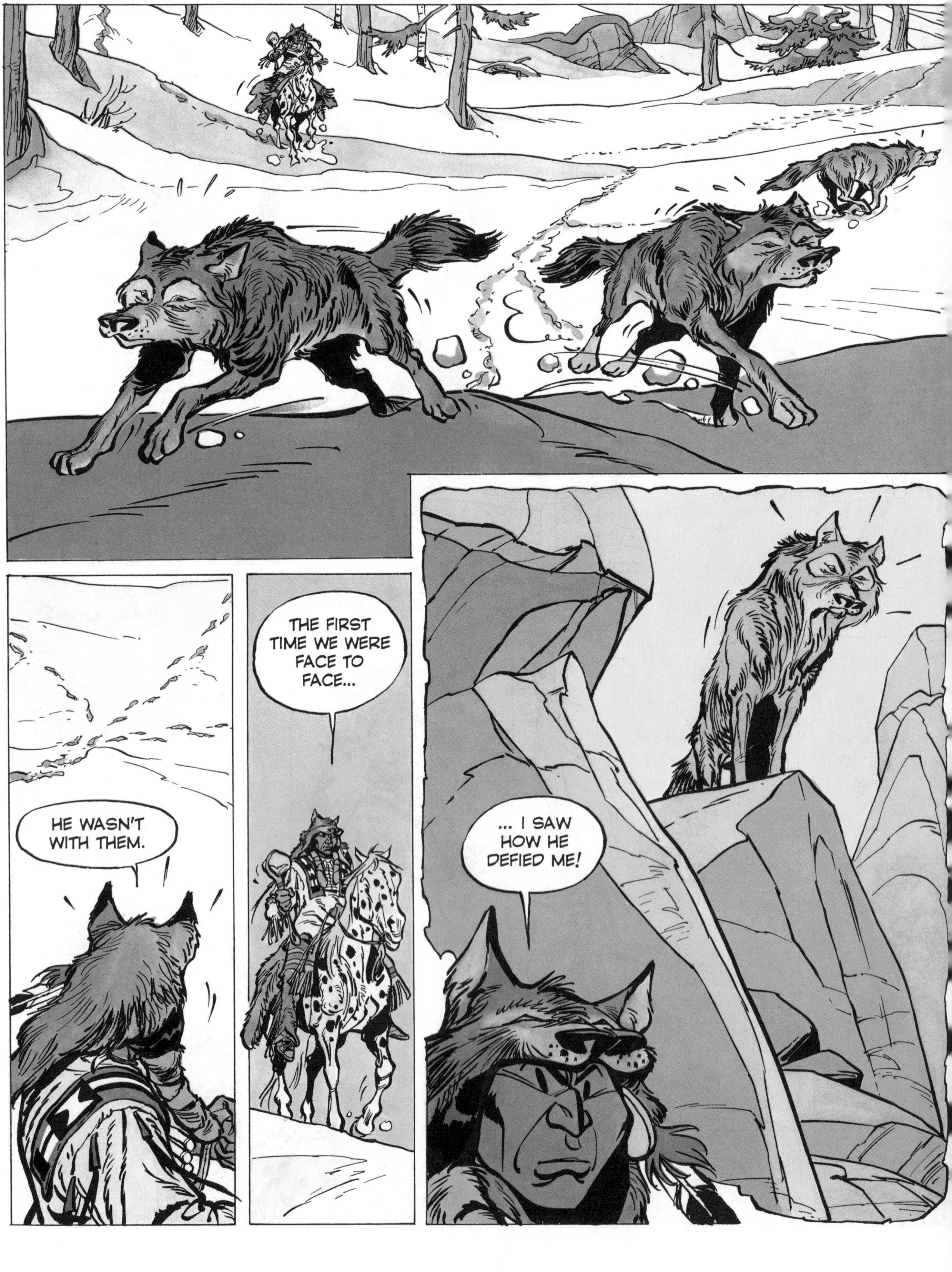
HE WASN'T WITH THEM.
THE FIRST TIME WE WERE FACE TO FACE...
... I SAW HOW HE DEFIED ME!

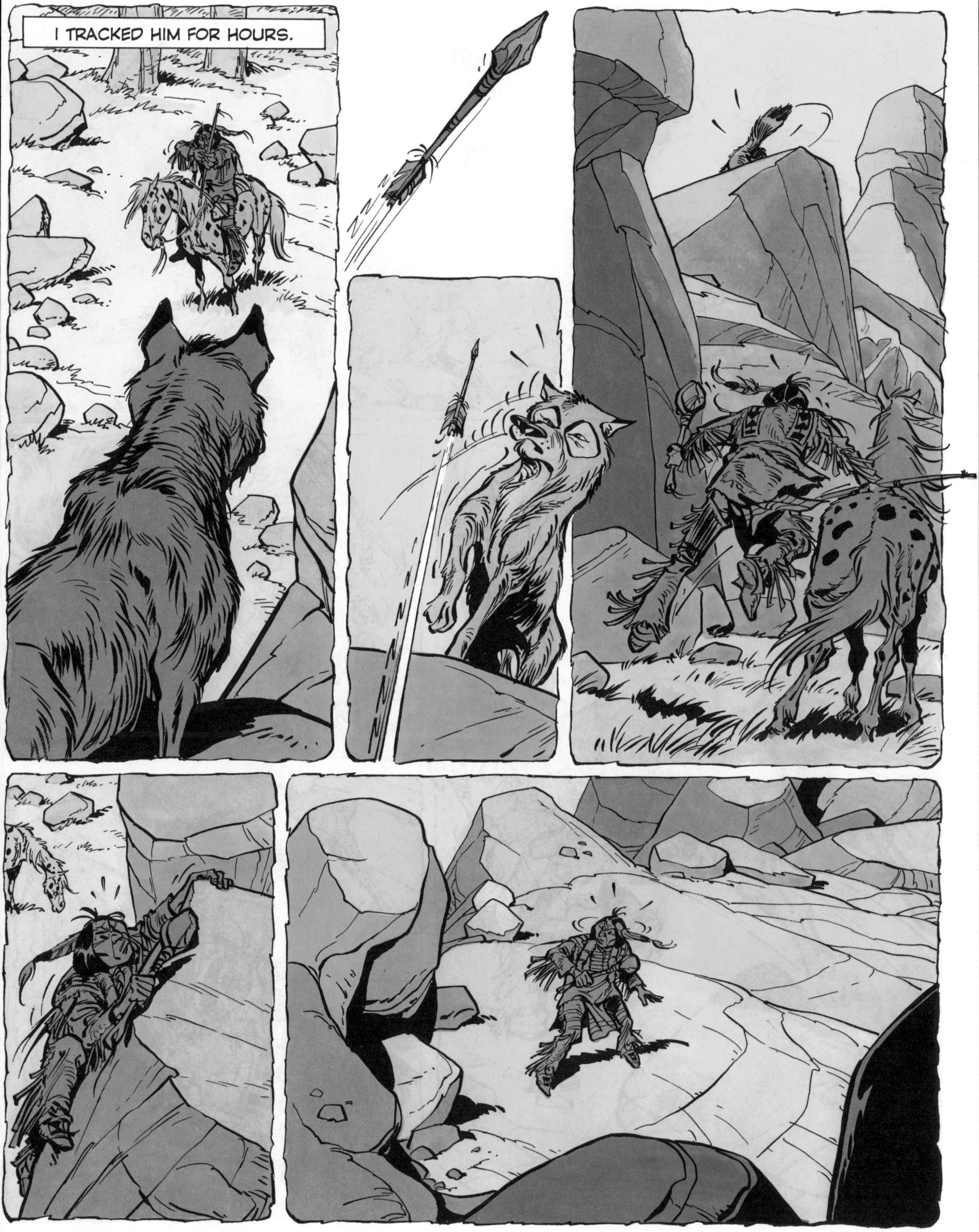
I TRACKED HIM FOR HOURS.

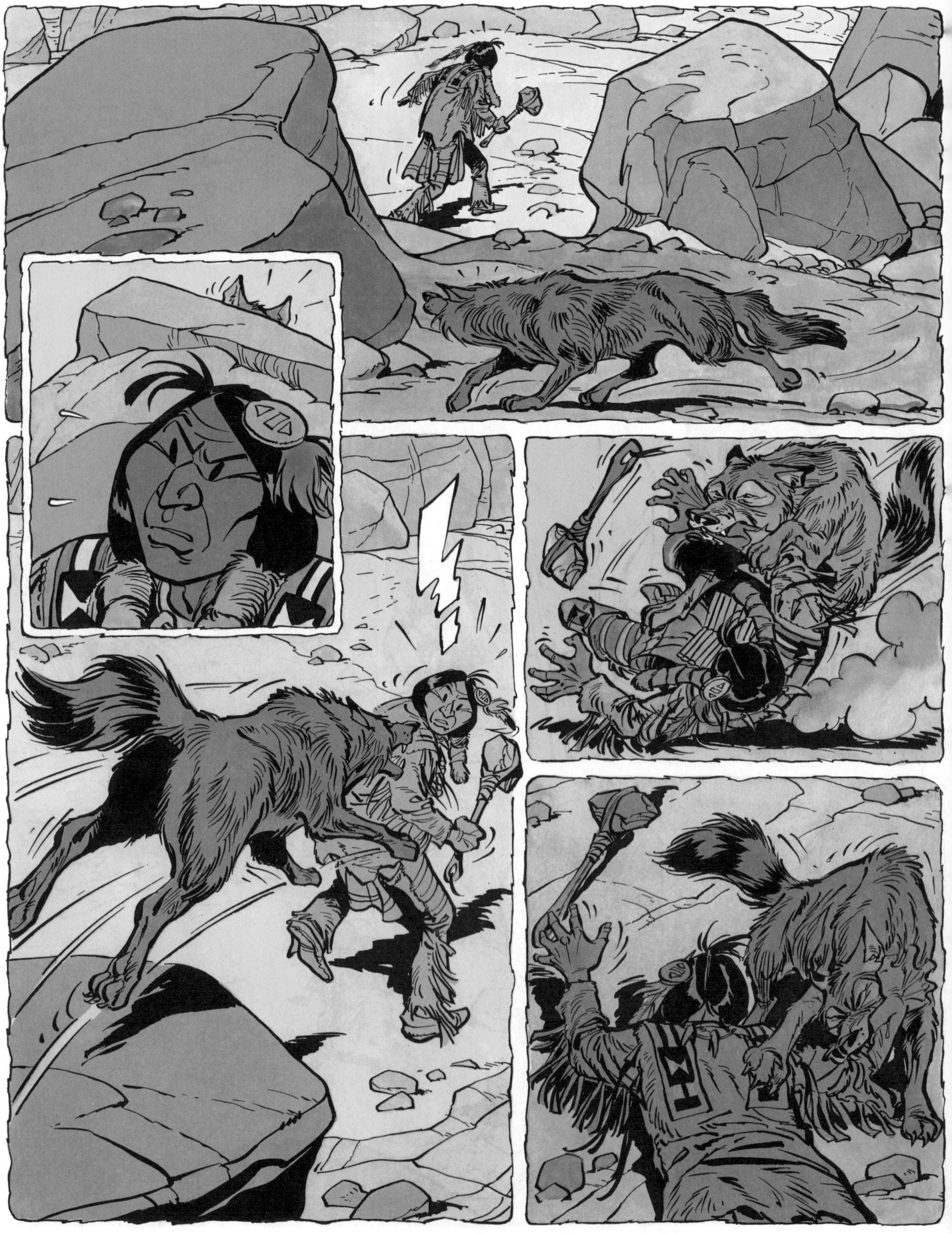

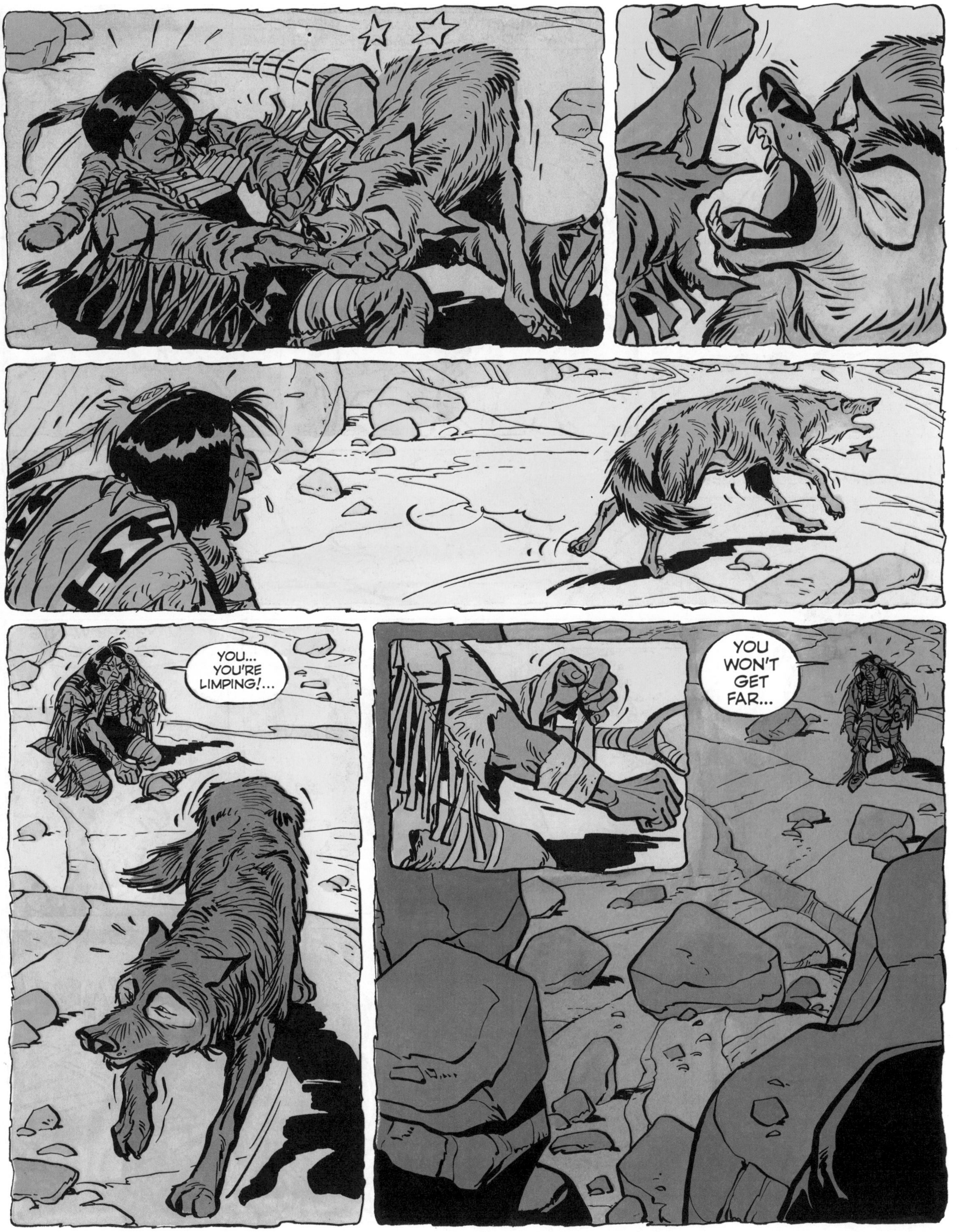
YOU... YOU'RE LIMPING!...
YOU WON'T GET FAR...

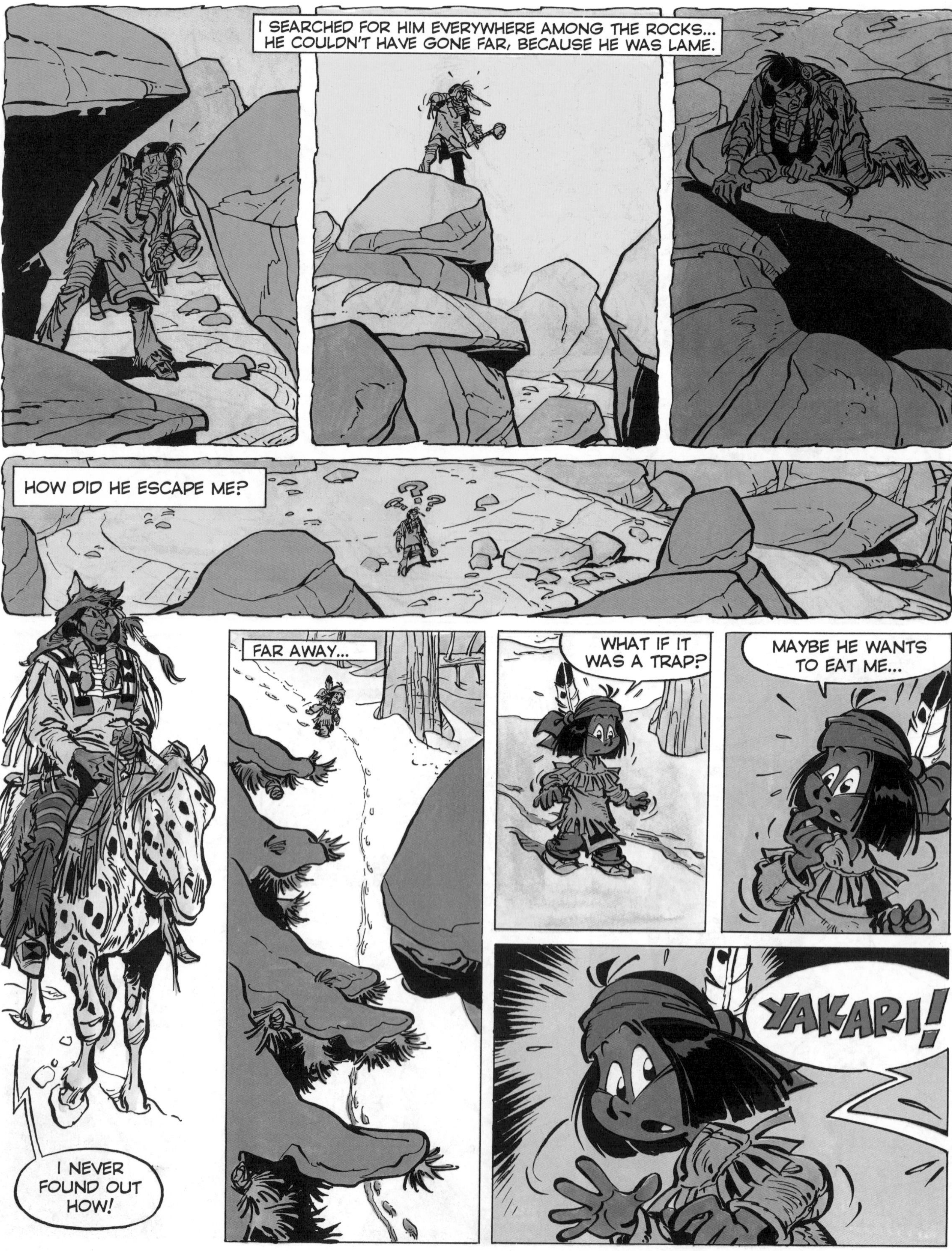
I SEARCHED FOR HIM EVERYWHERE AMONG THE ROCKS... HE COULDN'T HAVE GONE FAR, BECAUSE HE WAS LAME.
HOW DID HE ESCAPE ME?
I NEVER FOUND OUT HOW!
FAR AWAY...
WHAT IF IT WAS A TRAP?
MAYBE HE WANTS TO EAT ME...
YAKARI!

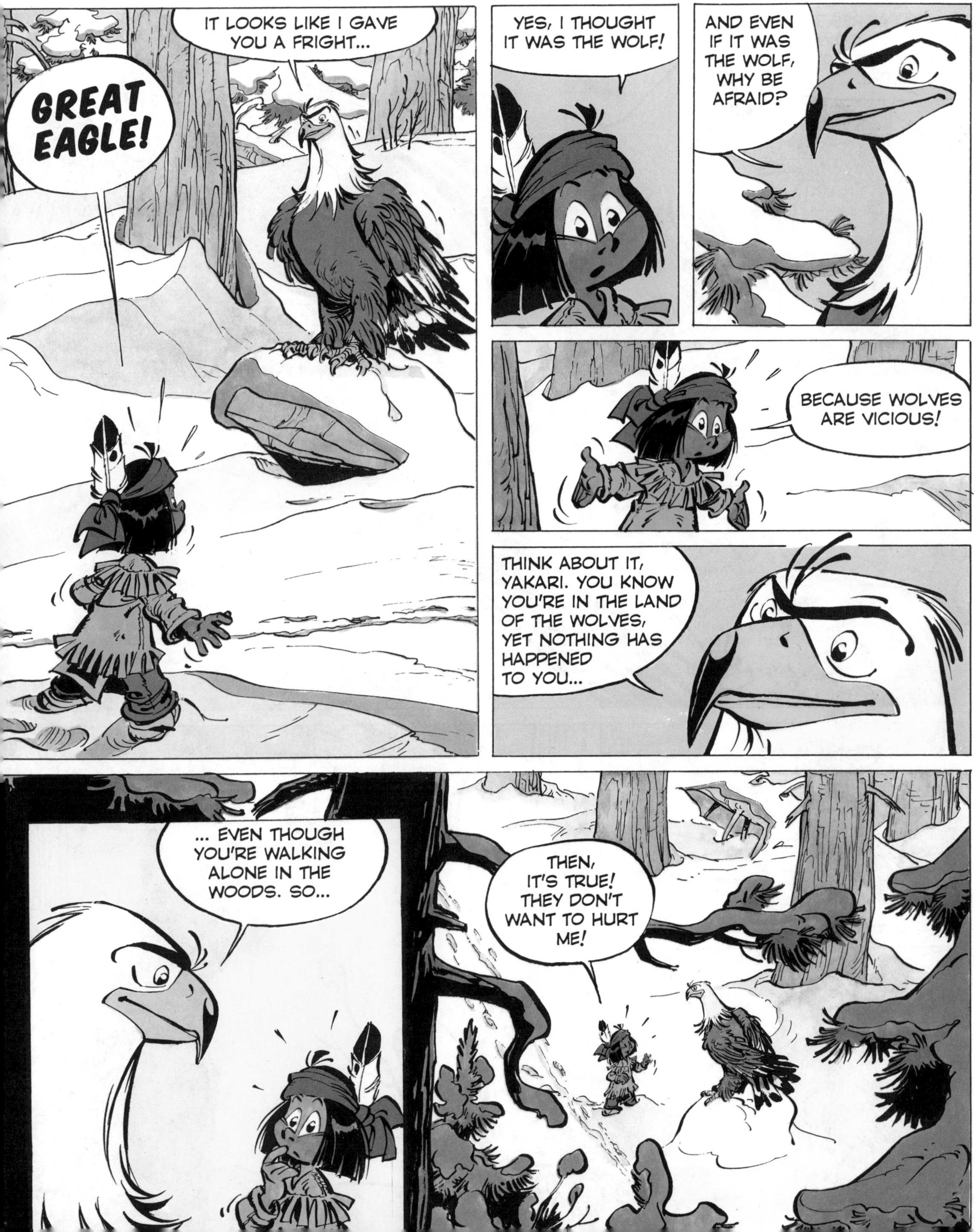

IT LOOKS LIKE I GAVE YOU A FRIGHT...
GREAT EAGLE!
YES, I THOUGHT IT WAS THE WOLF!
AND EVEN IF IT WAS THE WOLF, WHY BE AFRAID?
BECAUSE WOLVES ARE VICIOUS!
THINK ABOUT IT, YAKARI. YOU KNOW YOU'RE IN THE LAND OF THE WOLVES, YET NOTHING HAS HAPPENED TO YOU...
... EVEN THOUGH YOU'RE WALKING ALONE IN THE WOODS. SO...
THEN, IT'S TRUE! THEY DON'T WANT TO HURT ME!

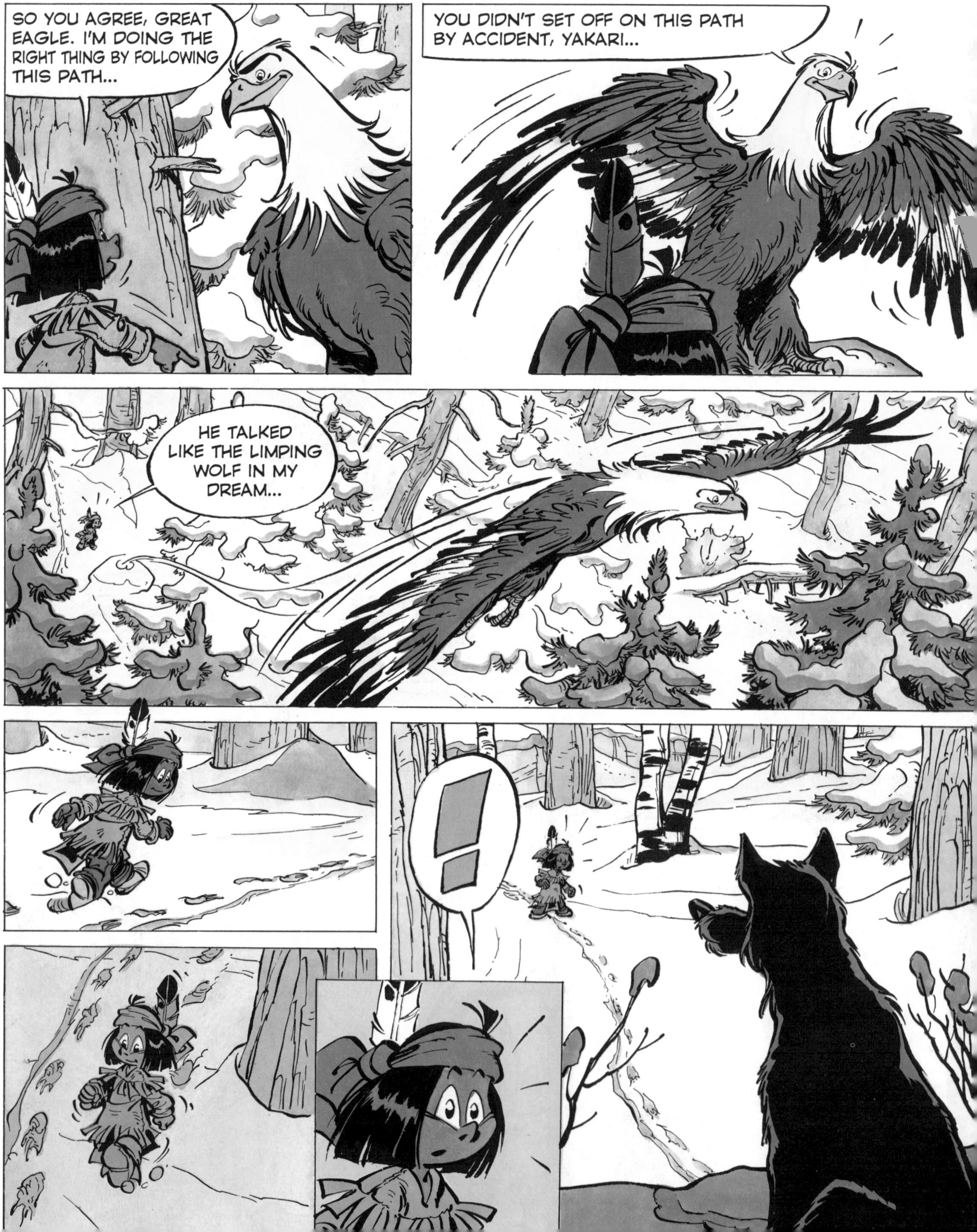
SO YOU AGREE, GREAT EAGLE. I'M DOING THE RIGHT THING BY FOLLOWING THIS PATH...
YOU DIDN'T SET OFF ON THIS PATH BY ACCIDENT, YAKARI...
HE TALKED LIKE THE LIMPING WOLF IN MY DREAM...
!
!

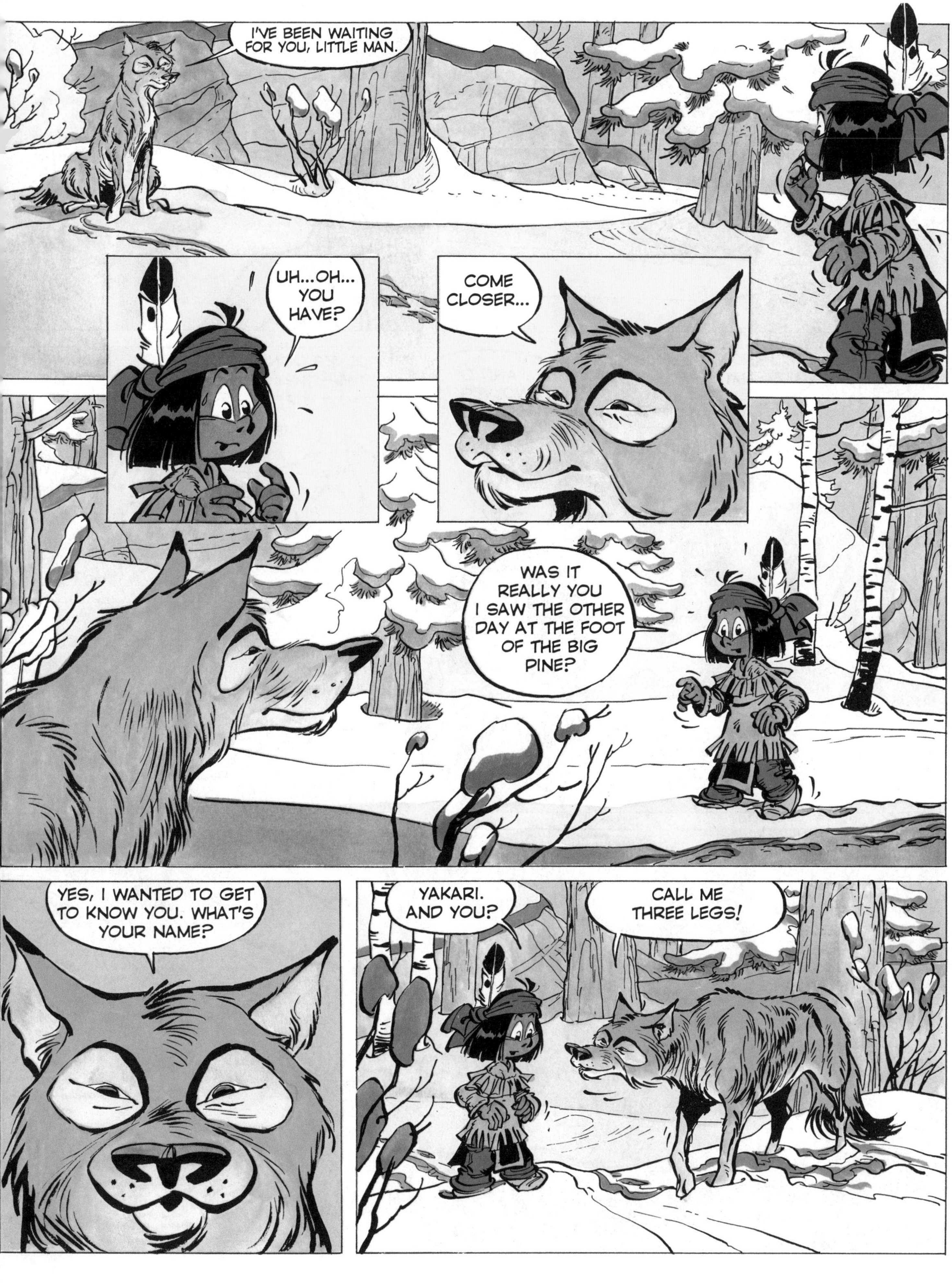
I'VE BEEN WAITING FOR YOU, LITTLE MAN.
UH...OH... YOU HAVE?
COME CLOSER...
WAS IT REALLY YOU I SAW THE OTHER DAY AT THE FOOT OF THE BIG PINE?
YES, I WANTED TO GET TO KNOW YOU. WHAT'S YOUR NAME?
YAKARI. AND YOU?
CALL ME THREE LEGS!

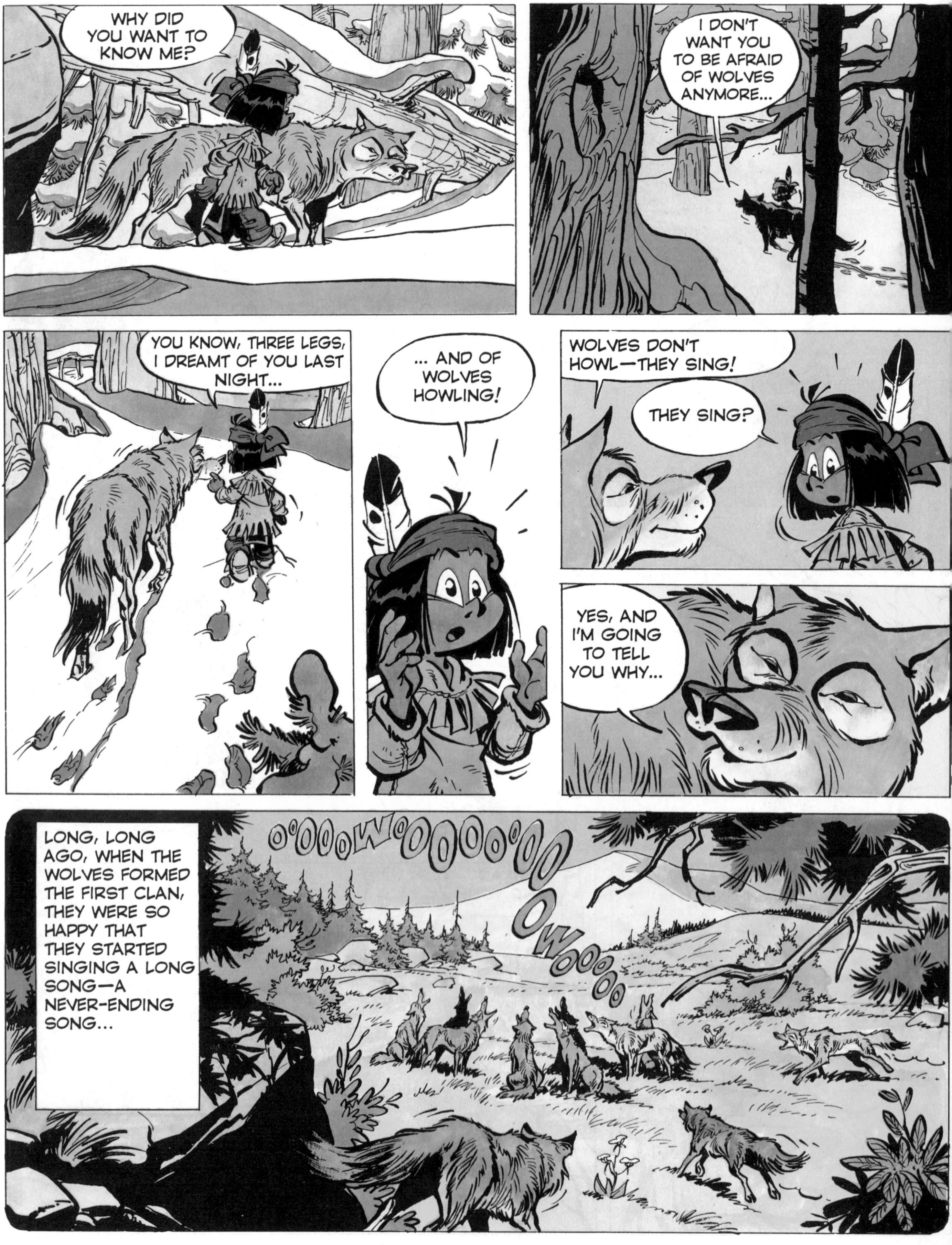

WHY DID YOU WANT TO KNOW ME?
I DON'T WANT YOU TO BE AFRAID OF WOLVES ANYMORE...
YOU KNOW, THREE LEGS, I DREAMT OF YOU LAST NIGHT...
... AND OF WOLVES HOWLING!
WOLVES DON'T HOWL—THEY SING!
THEY SING?
YES, AND I'M GOING TO TELL YOU WHY...
LONG, LONG AGO, WHEN THE WOLVES FORMED THE FIRST CLAN, THEY WERE SO HAPPY THAT THEY STARTED SINGING A LONG SONG—A NEVER-ENDING SONG...
O°OOOWOOOOOO°OOOOWOOOOO

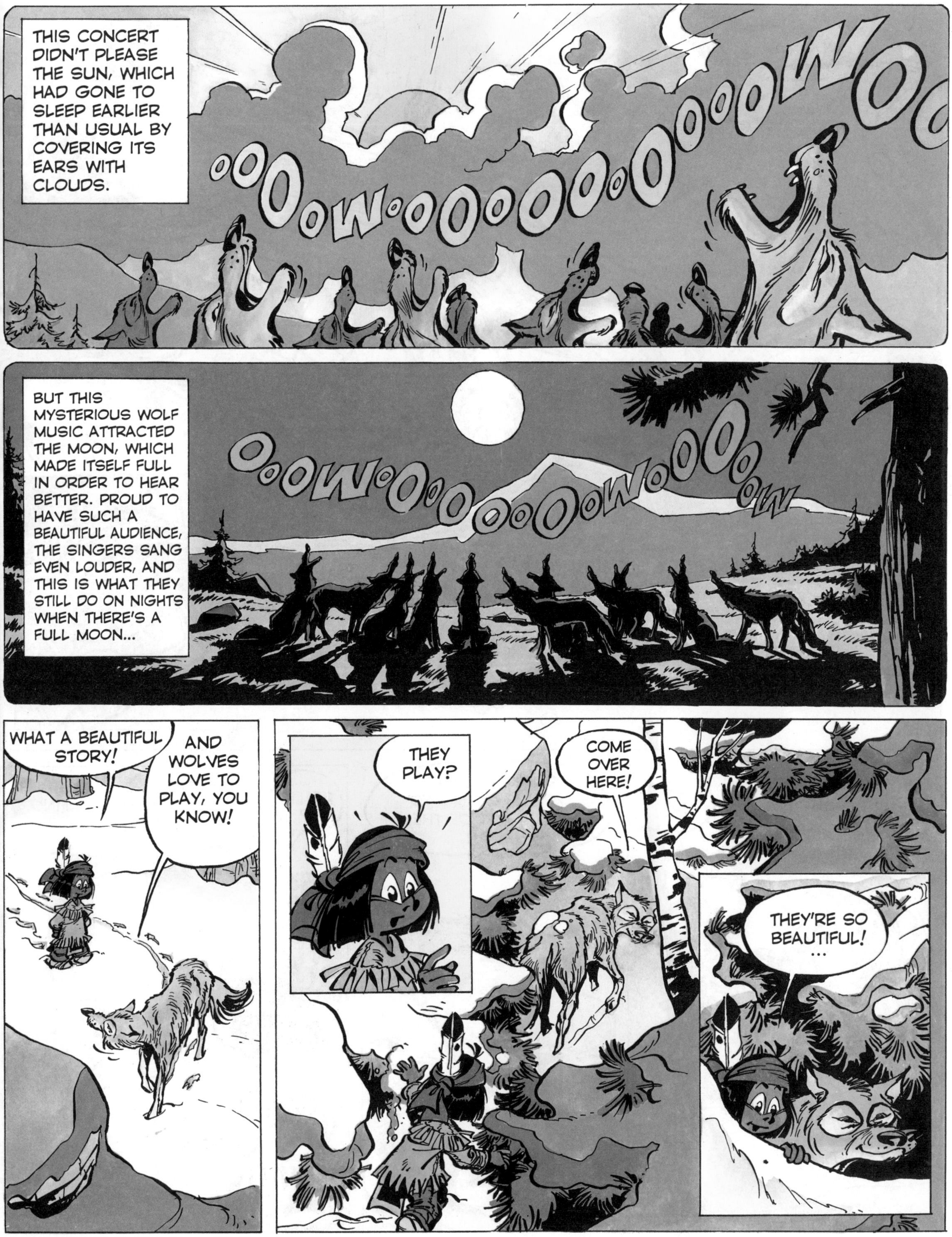
THIS CONCERT DIDN'T PLEASE THE SUN, WHICH HAD GONE TO SLEEP EARLIER THAN USUAL BY COVERING ITS EARS WITH CLOUDS.
BUT THIS MYSTERIOUS WOLF MUSIC ATTRACTED THE MOON, WHICH MADE ITSELF FULL IN ORDER TO HEAR BETTER. PROUD TO HAVE SUCH A BEAUTIFUL AUDIENCE, THE SINGERS SANG EVEN LOUDER, AND THIS IS WHAT THEY STILL DO ON NIGHTS WHEN THERE'S A FULL MOON...
WHAT A BEAUTIFUL STORY!
AND WOLVES LOVE TO PLAY, YOU KNOW!
THEY PLAY?
COME OVER HERE!
THEY'RE SO BEAUTIFUL! ...

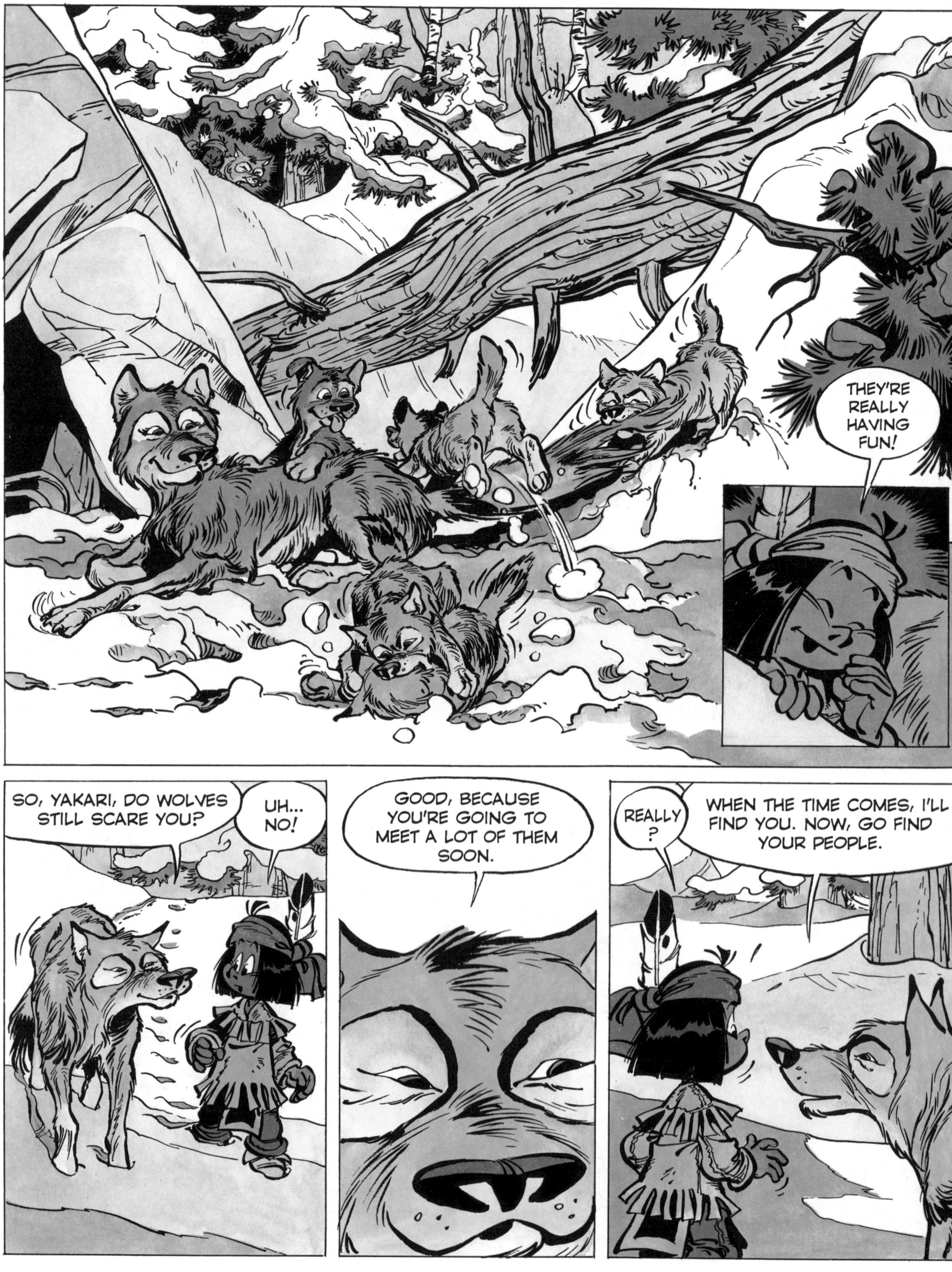
THEY'RE REALLY HAVING FUN!
SO, YAKARI, DO WOLVES STILL SCARE YOU?
UH... NO!
GOOD, BECAUSE YOU'RE GOING TO MEET A LOT OF THEM SOON.
REALLY?
WHEN THE TIME COMES, I'LL FIND YOU. NOW, GO FIND YOUR PEOPLE.

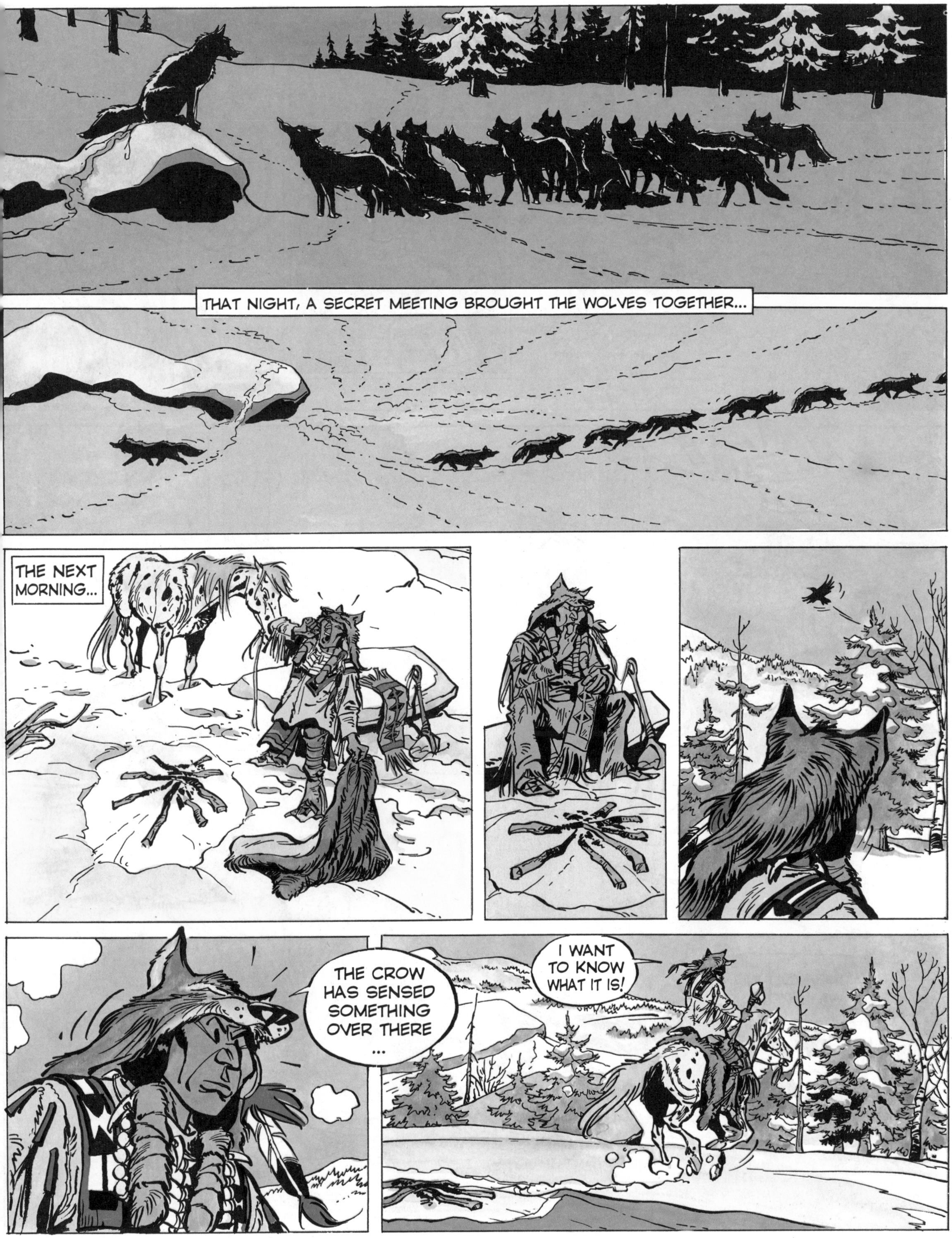
THAT NIGHT, A SECRET MEETING BROUGHT THE WOLVES TOGETHER...
THE NEXT MORNING...
THE CROW HAS SENSED SOMETHING OVER THERE ...
I WANT TO KNOW WHAT IT IS!

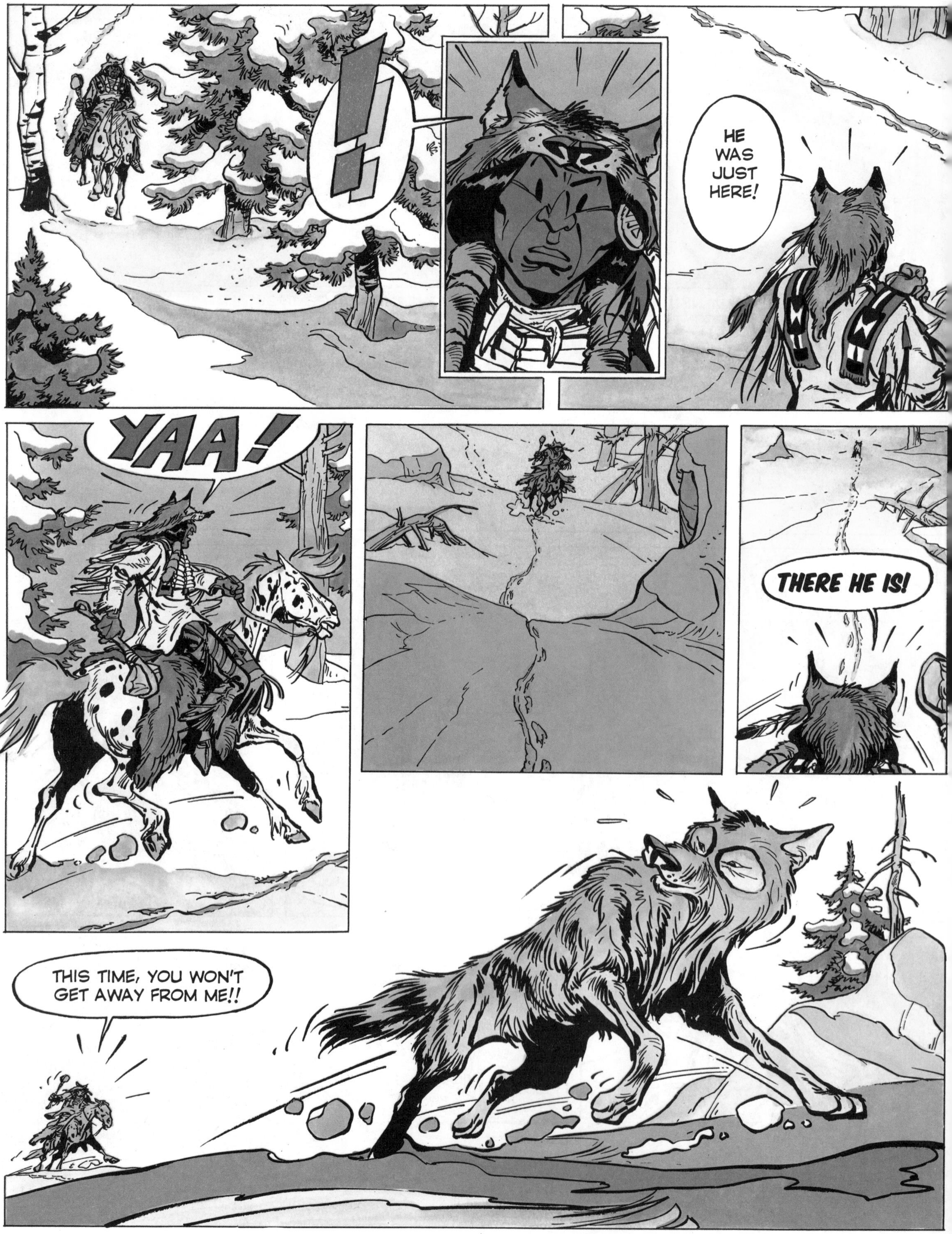

!!
HE WAS JUST HERE!
YAA!
THERE HE IS!
THIS TIME, YOU WON'T GET AWAY FROM ME!!

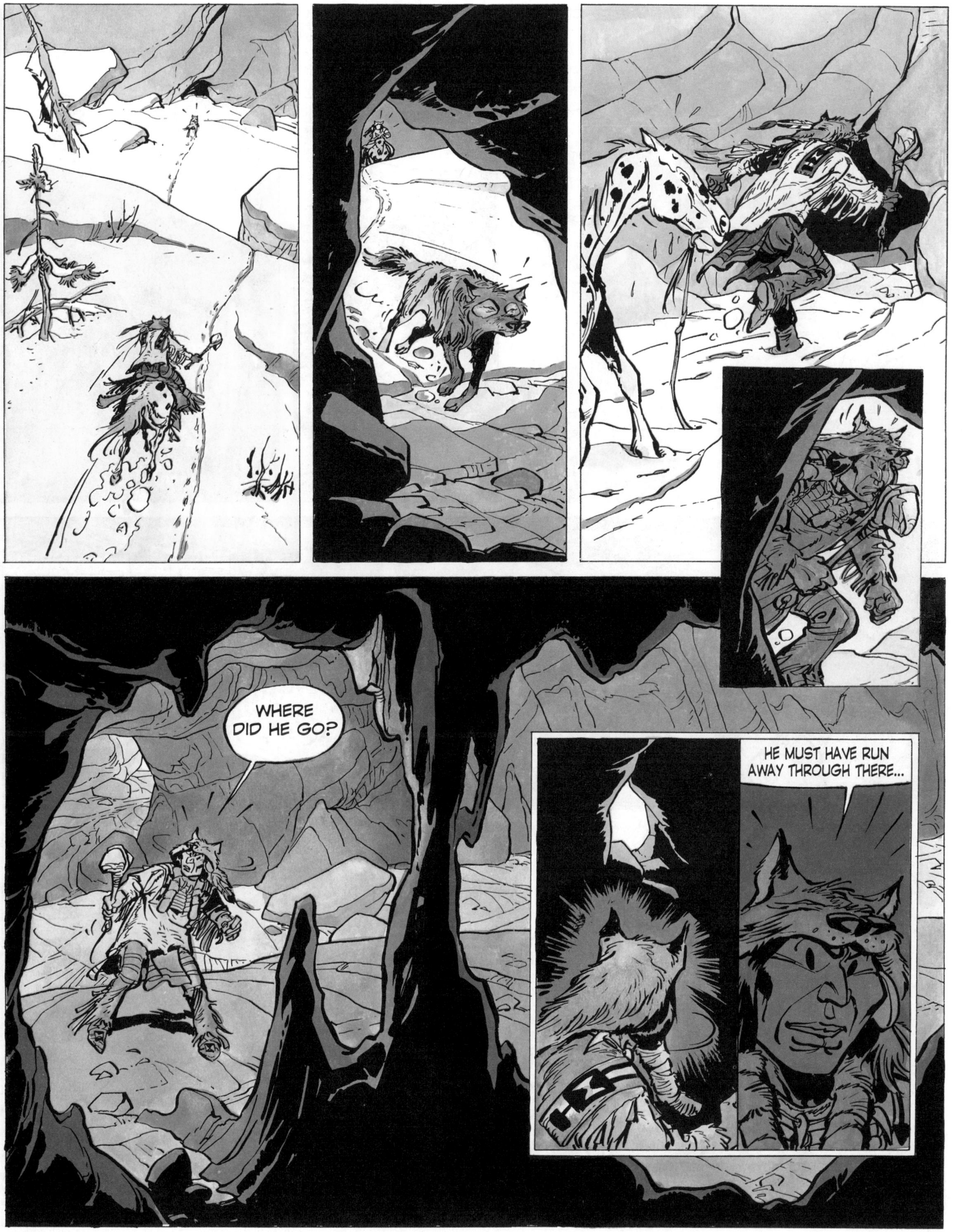
WHERE DID HE GO?
HE MUST HAVE RUN AWAY THROUGH THERE...

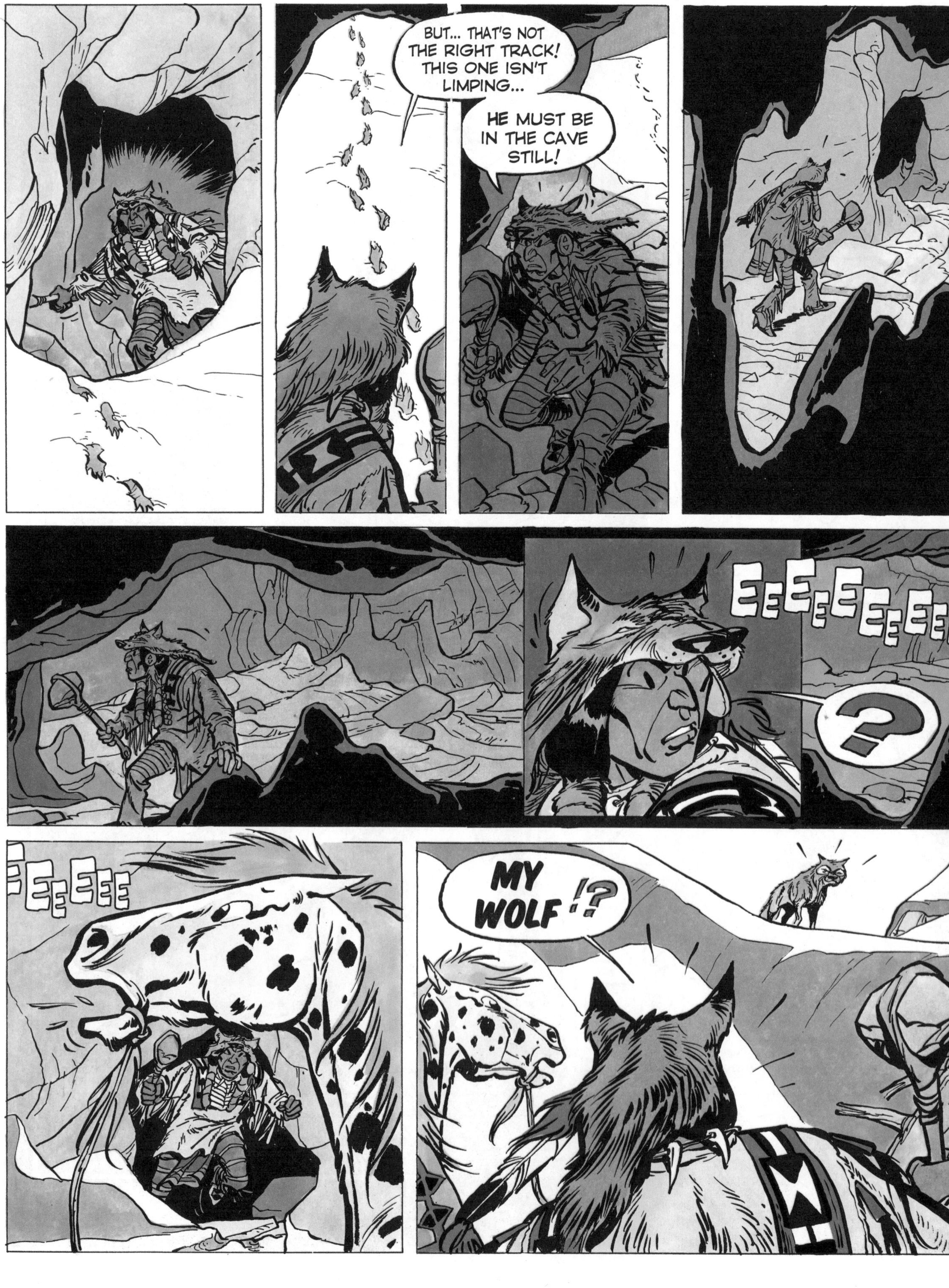
BUT... THAT'S NOT THE RIGHT TRACK! THIS ONE ISN'T LIMPING...
HE MUST BE IN THE CAVE STILL!
EEEEEEEEEEE
?
EEEEEE
MY WOLF !?

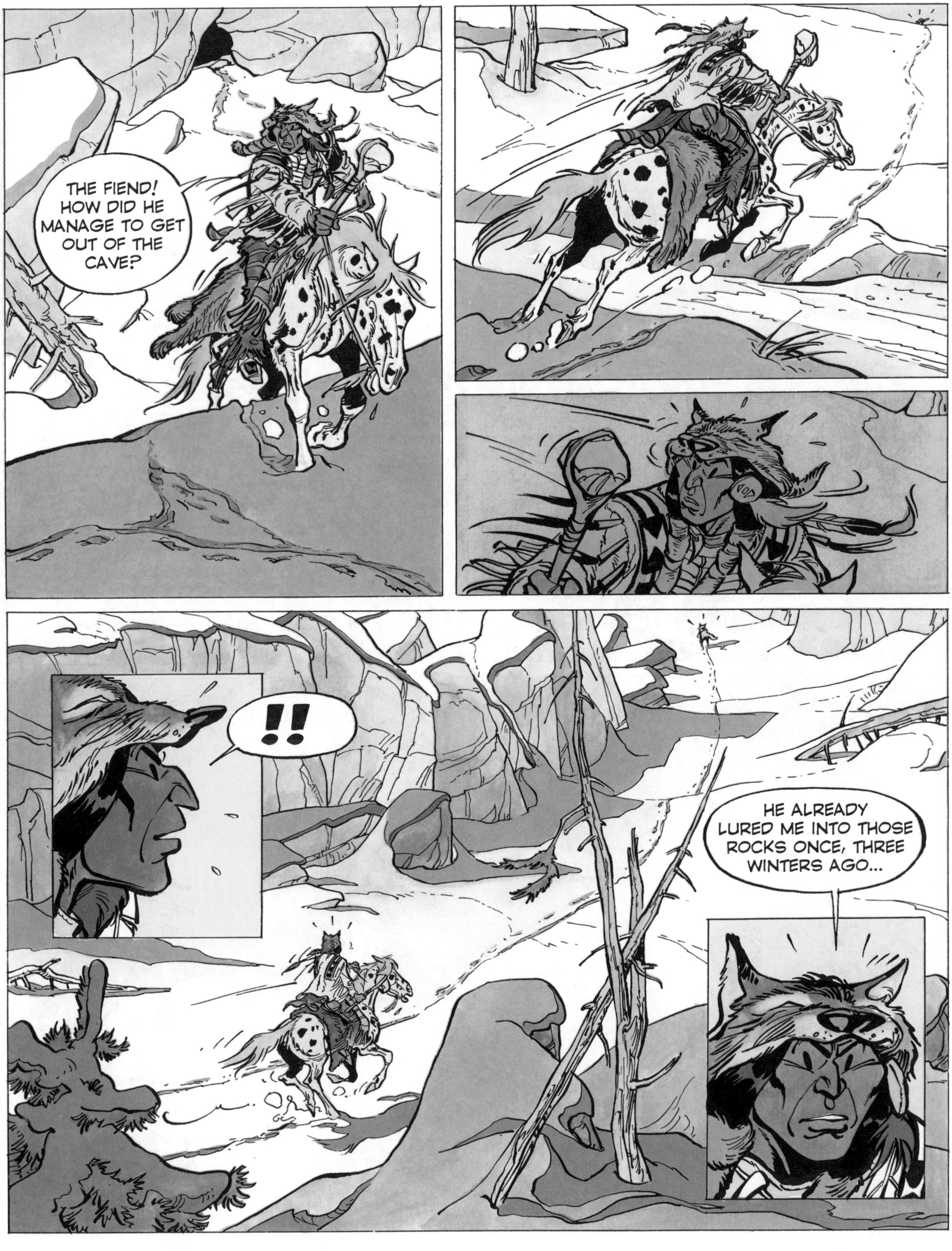
THE FIEND! HOW DID HE MANAGE TO GET OUT OF THE CAVE?
!!
HE ALREADY LURED ME INTO THOSE ROCKS ONCE, THREE WINTERS AGO...

SO, THIS IS WHERE YOU WANT TO FIGHT?...

I'M COMING!

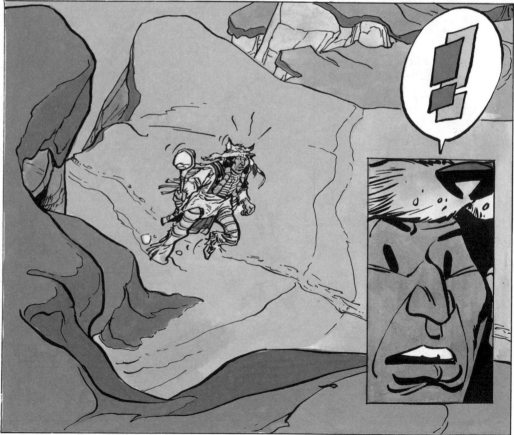

38

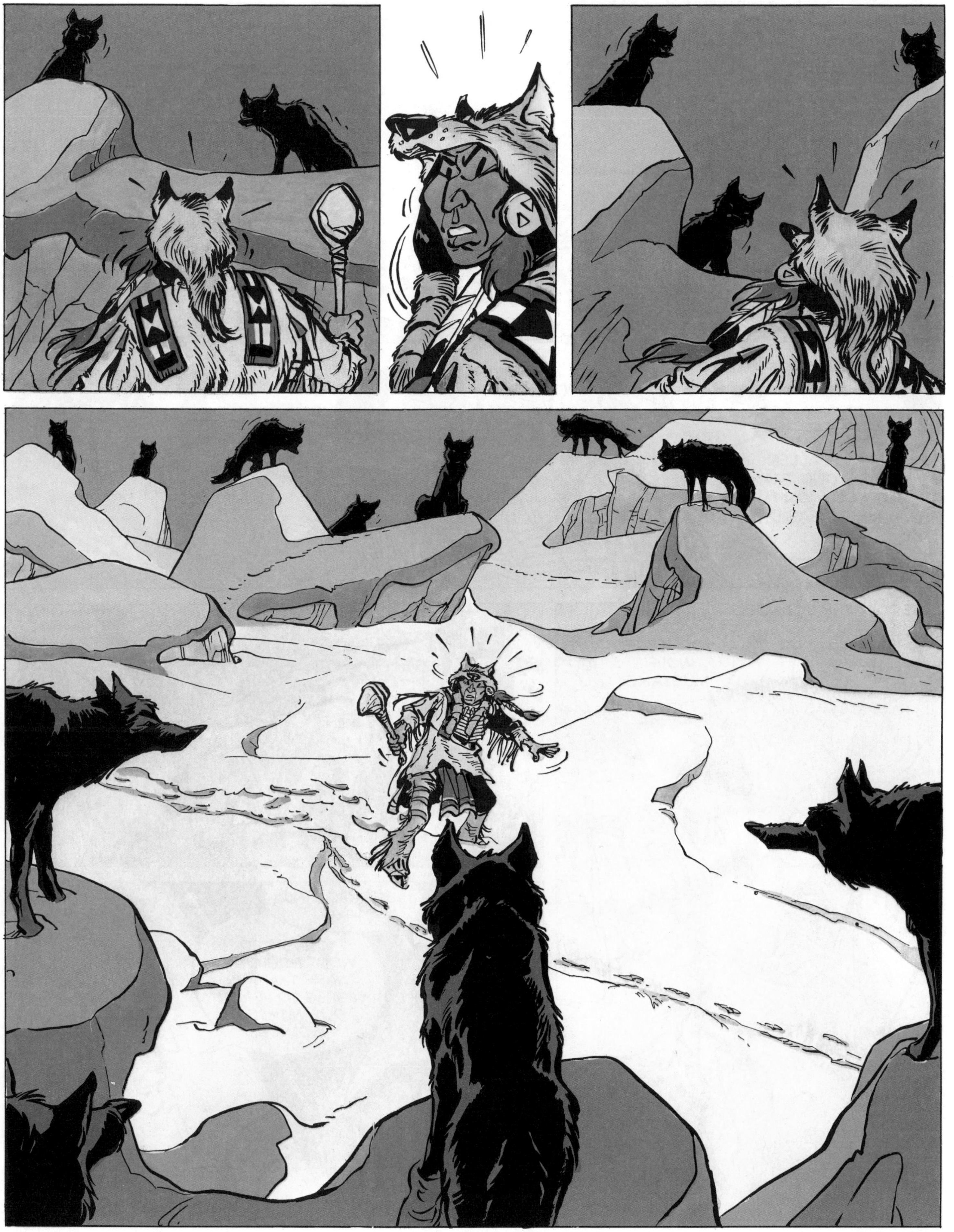

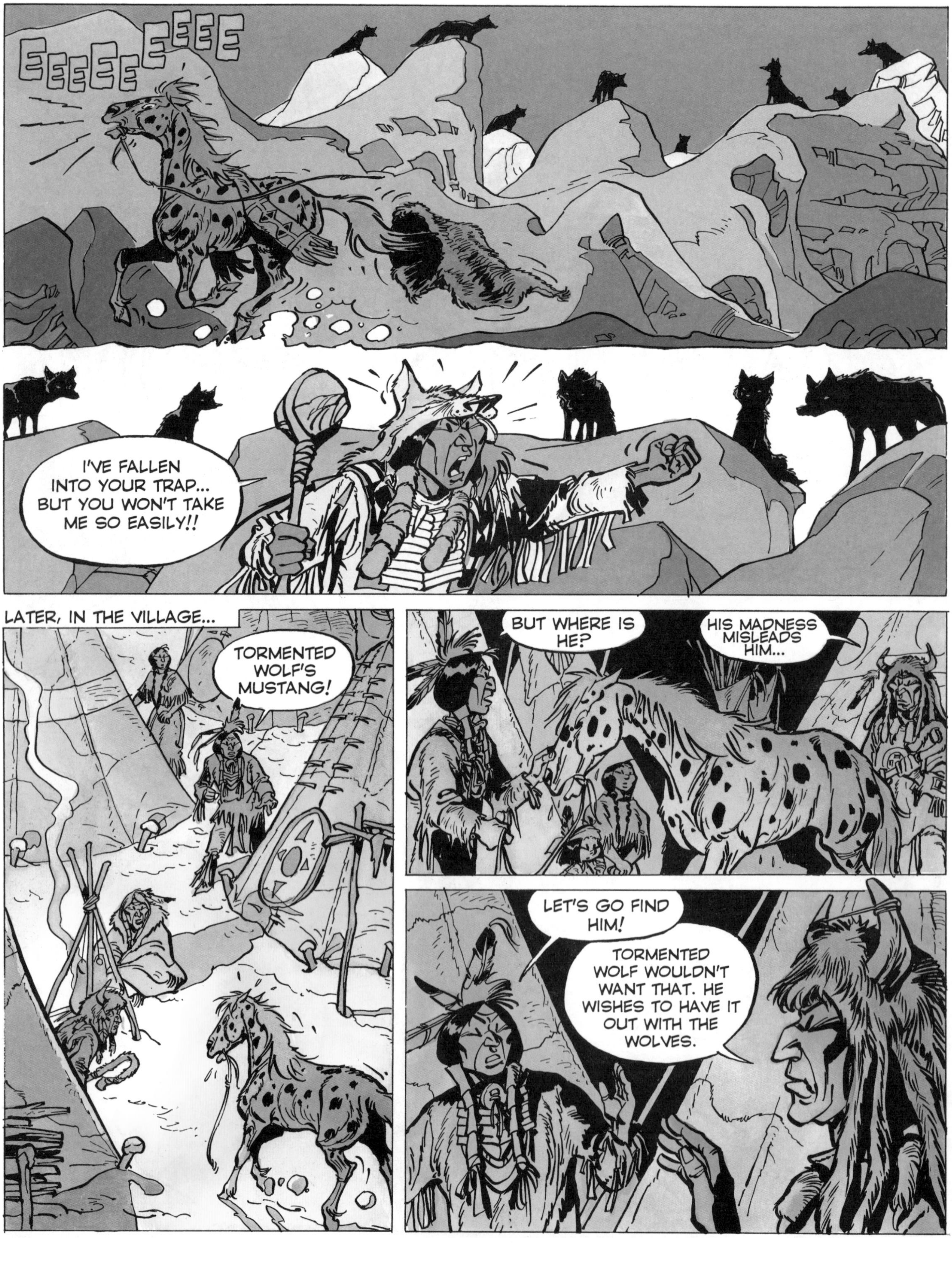
EEEEEEEEEE
I'VE FALLEN INTO YOUR TRAP... BUT YOU WON'T TAKE ME SO EASILY!!
LATER, IN THE VILLAGE...
TORMENTED WOLF'S MUSTANG!
BUT WHERE IS HE?
HIS MADNESS MISLEADS HIM...
LET'S GO FIND HIM!
TORMENTED WOLF WOULDN'T WANT THAT. HE WISHES TO HAVE IT OUT WITH THE WOLVES.

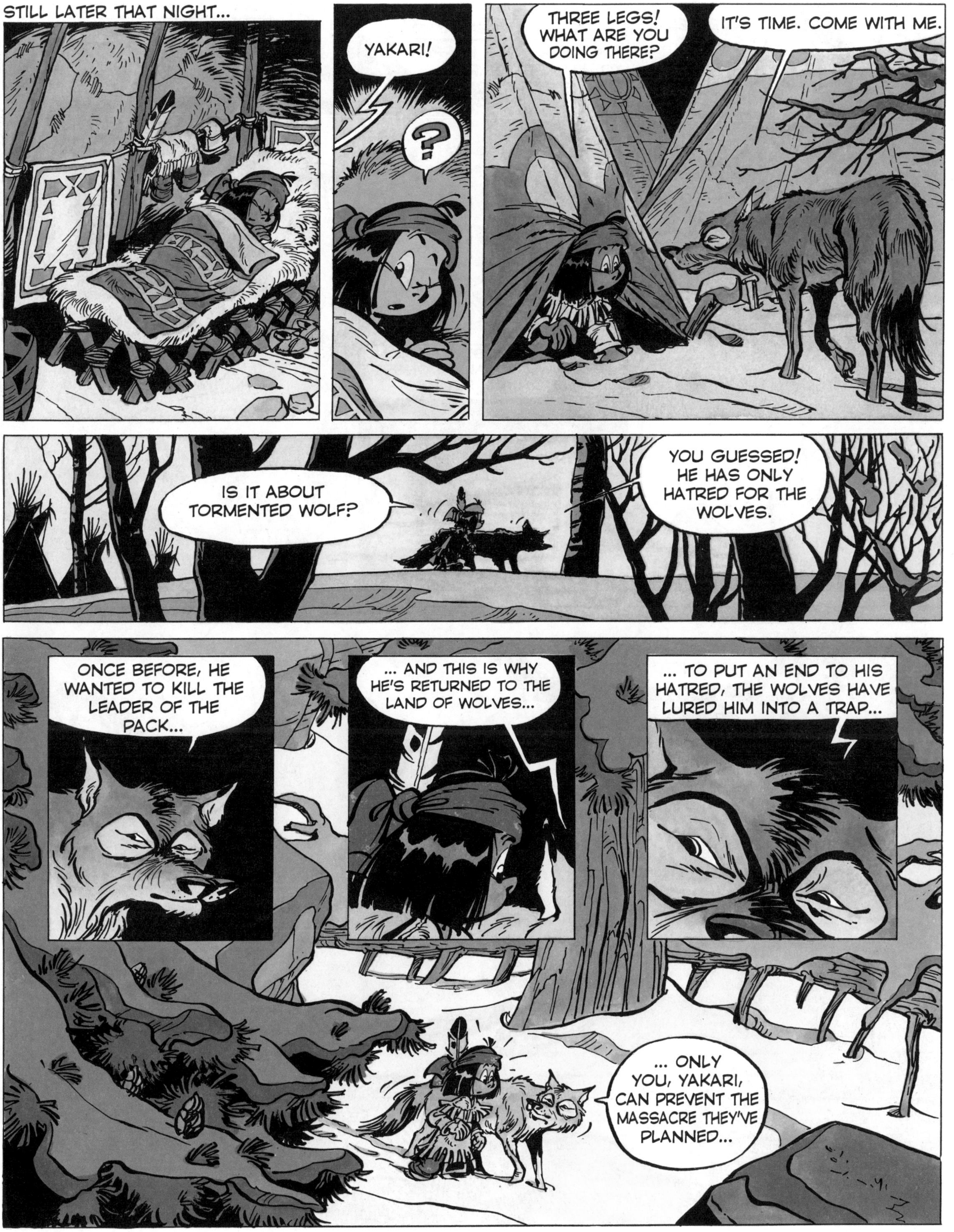
STILL LATER THAT NIGHT...
YAKARI!
?
THREE LEGS! WHAT ARE YOU DOING THERE?
IT'S TIME. COME WITH ME.
IS IT ABOUT TORMENTED WOLF?
YOU GUESSED! HE HAS ONLY HATRED FOR THE WOLVES.
ONCE BEFORE, HE WANTED TO KILL THE LEADER OF THE PACK...
... AND THIS IS WHY HE'S RETURNED TO THE LAND OF WOLVES...
... TO PUT AN END TO HIS HATRED, THE WOLVES HAVE LURED HIM INTO A TRAP...
... ONLY YOU, YAKARI, CAN PREVENT THE MASSACRE THEY'VE PLANNED...

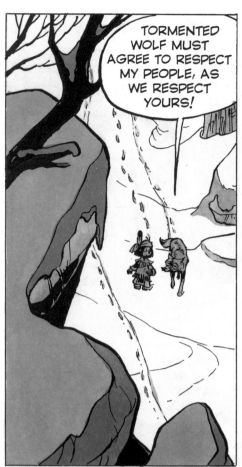

TORMENTED WOLF MUST AGREE TO RESPECT MY PEOPLE, AS WE RESPECT YOURS!

YOUR MISSION IS TO GET HIM TO UNDERSTAND THIS.

AND WHAT WILL HAPPEN TO HIM AFTERWARD?

AS A SIGN OF SUBMISSION, HE'LL HAVE TO WALK AMONGST US ON ALL FOURS.

IT'S THE ONLY WAY HE'LL SAVE HIS LIFE! IT'S WHAT THE LEADER OF THE WOLVES WANTS!

WE'RE HERE!

GO TALK WITH TORMENTED WOLF!

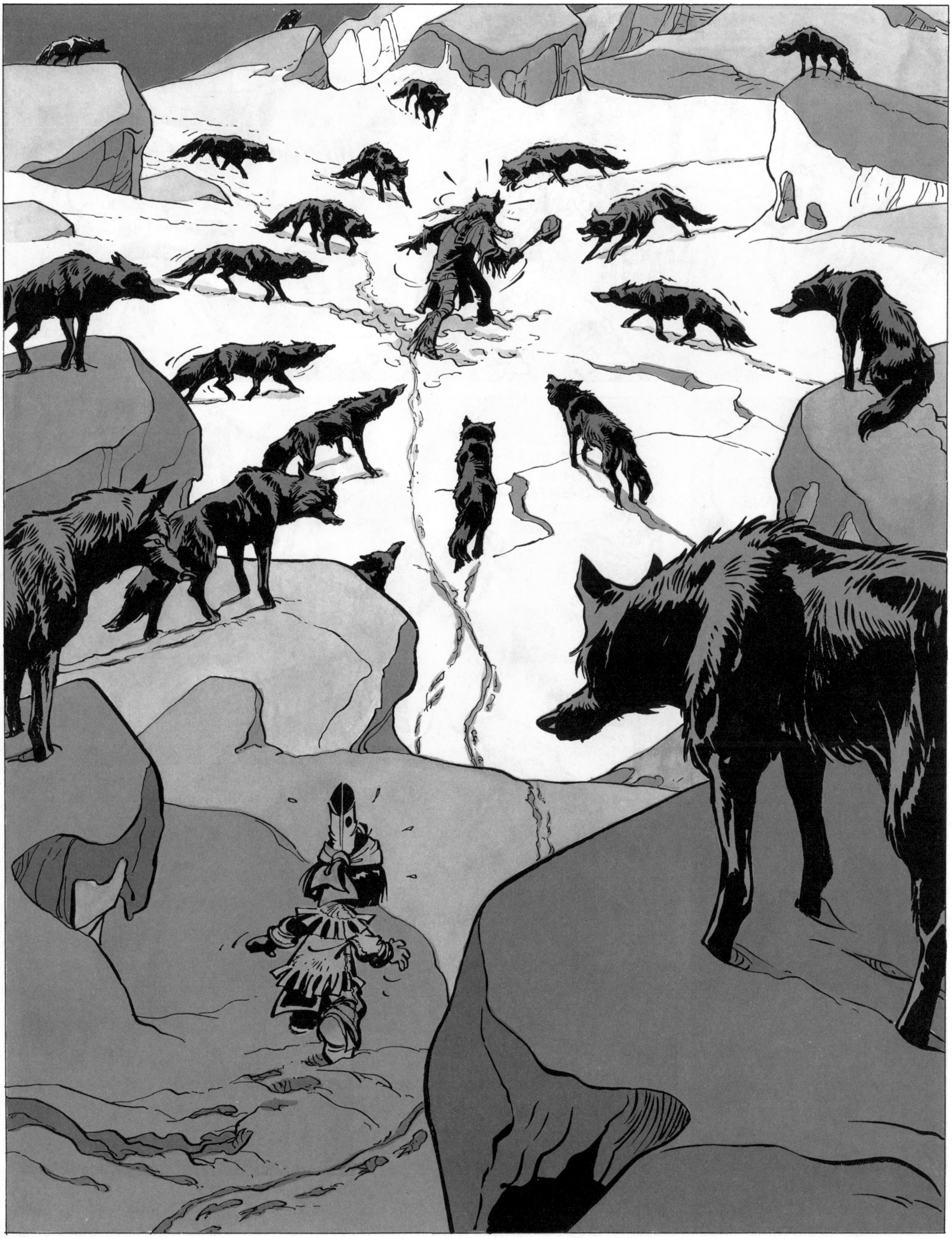

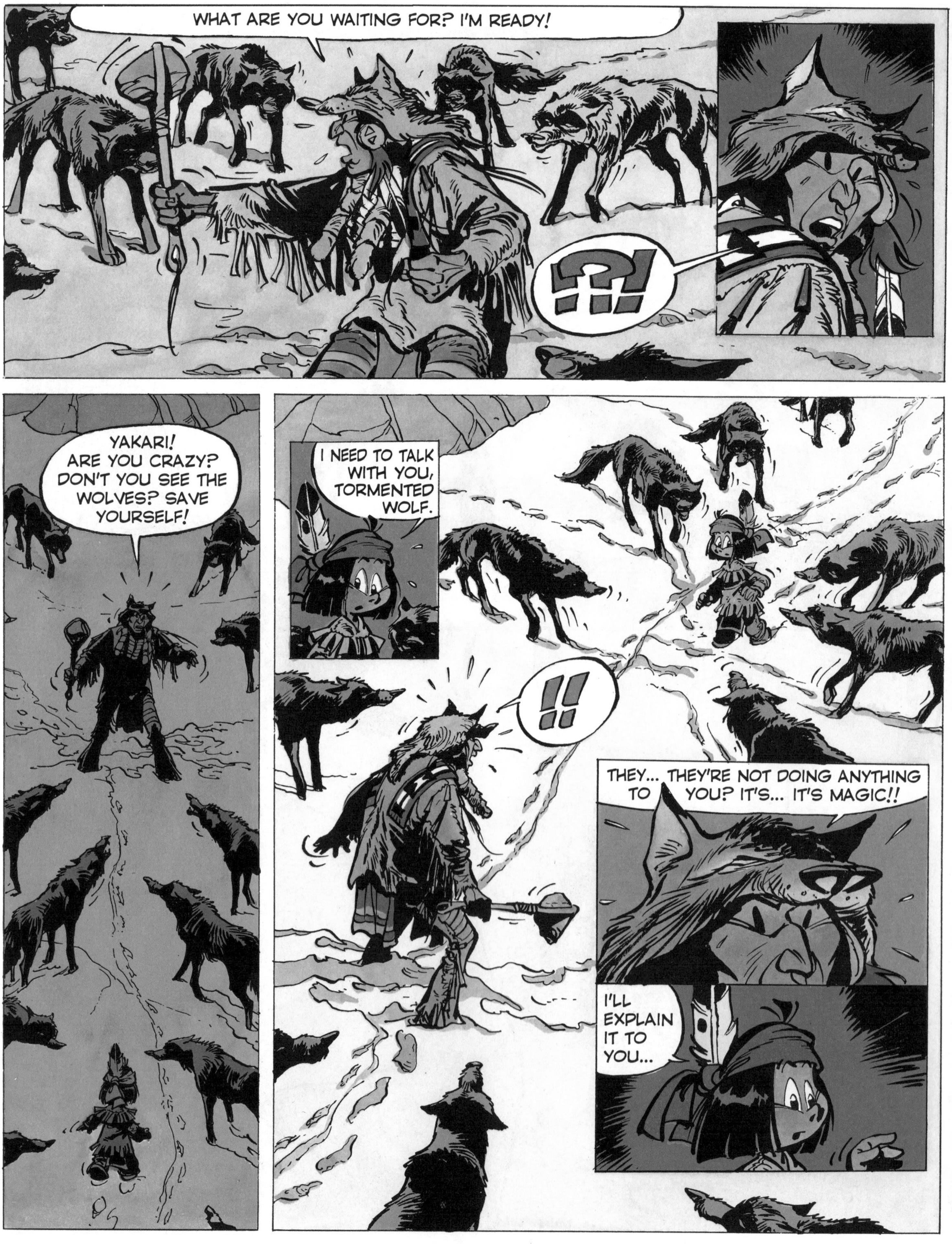
WHAT ARE YOU WAITING FOR? I'M READY!
?!
YAKARI! ARE YOU CRAZY? DON'T YOU SEE THE WOLVES? SAVE YOURSELF!
I NEED TO TALK WITH YOU, TORMENTED WOLF.
!!
THEY... THEY'RE NOT DOING ANYTHING TO YOU? IT'S... IT'S MAGIC!!
I'LL EXPLAIN IT TO YOU...

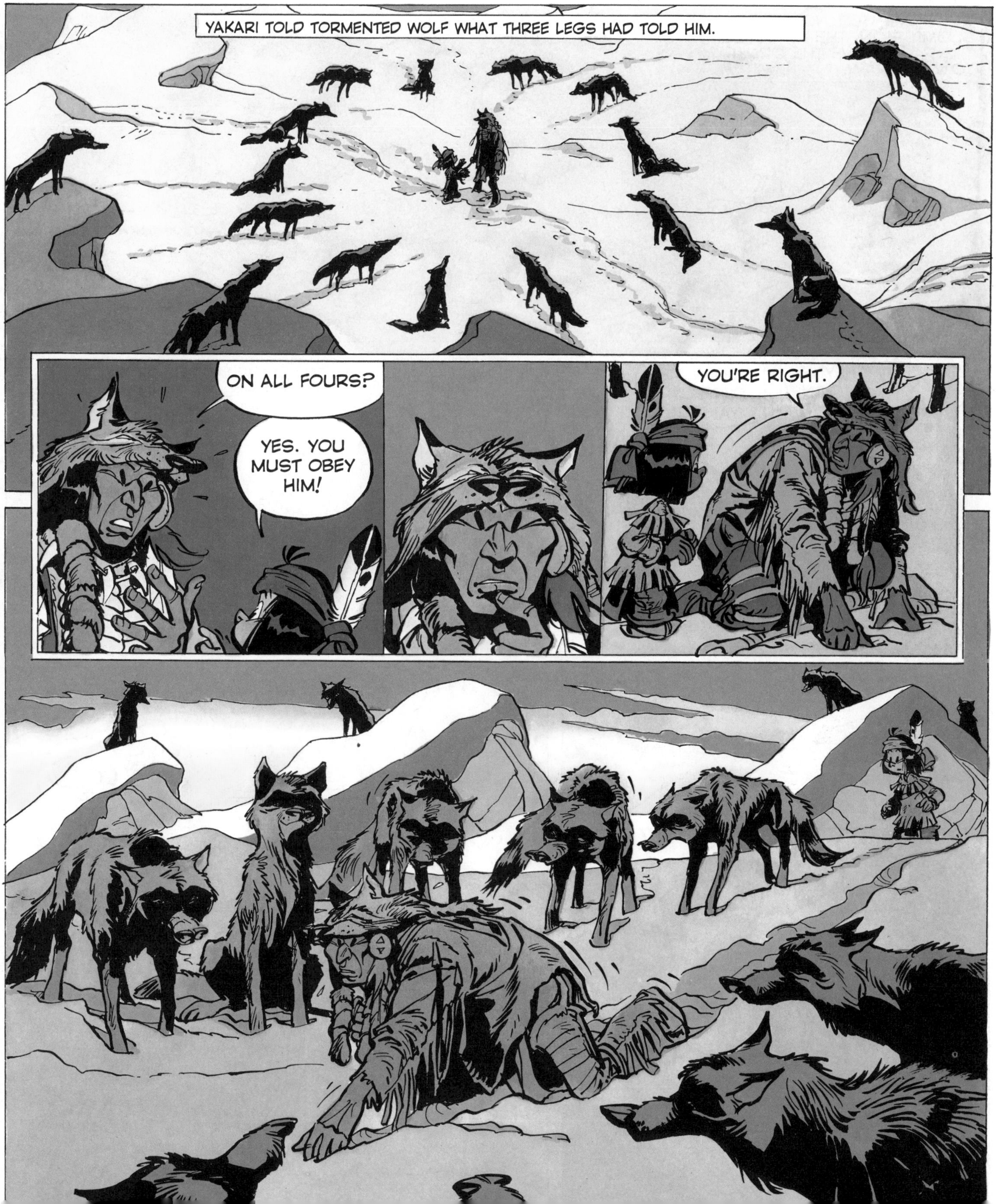

YAKARI TOLD TORMENTED WOLF WHAT THREE LEGS HAD TOLD HIM.
ON ALL FOURS?
YES. YOU MUST OBEY HIM!
YOU'RE RIGHT.

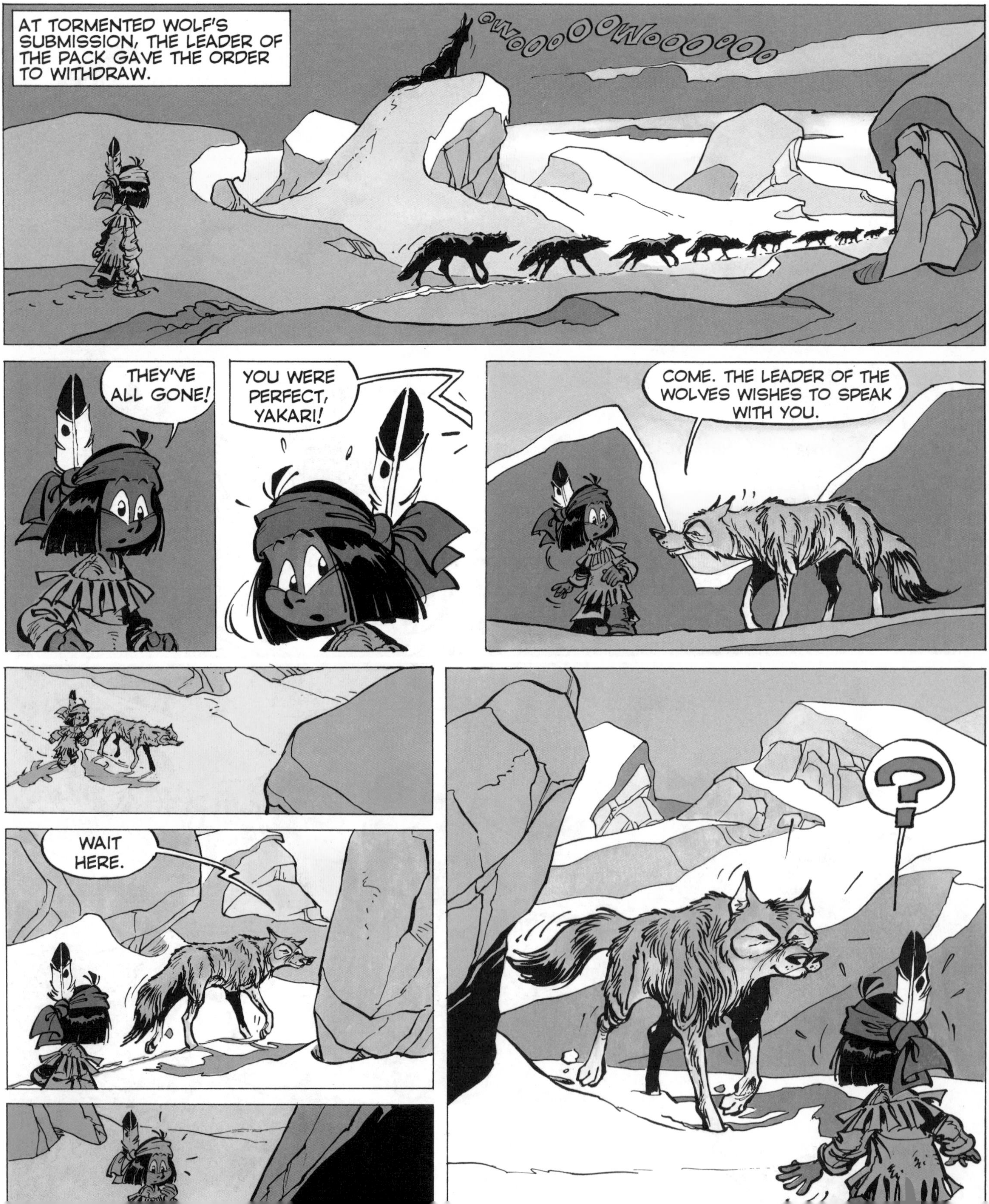
AT TORMENTED WOLF'S SUBMISSION, THE LEADER OF THE PACK GAVE THE ORDER TO WITHDRAW.
OWOOOOOWOOOOOOO
THEY'VE ALL GONE!
YOU WERE PERFECT, YAKARI!
COME. THE LEADER OF THE WOLVES WISHES TO SPEAK WITH YOU.
WAIT HERE.
?

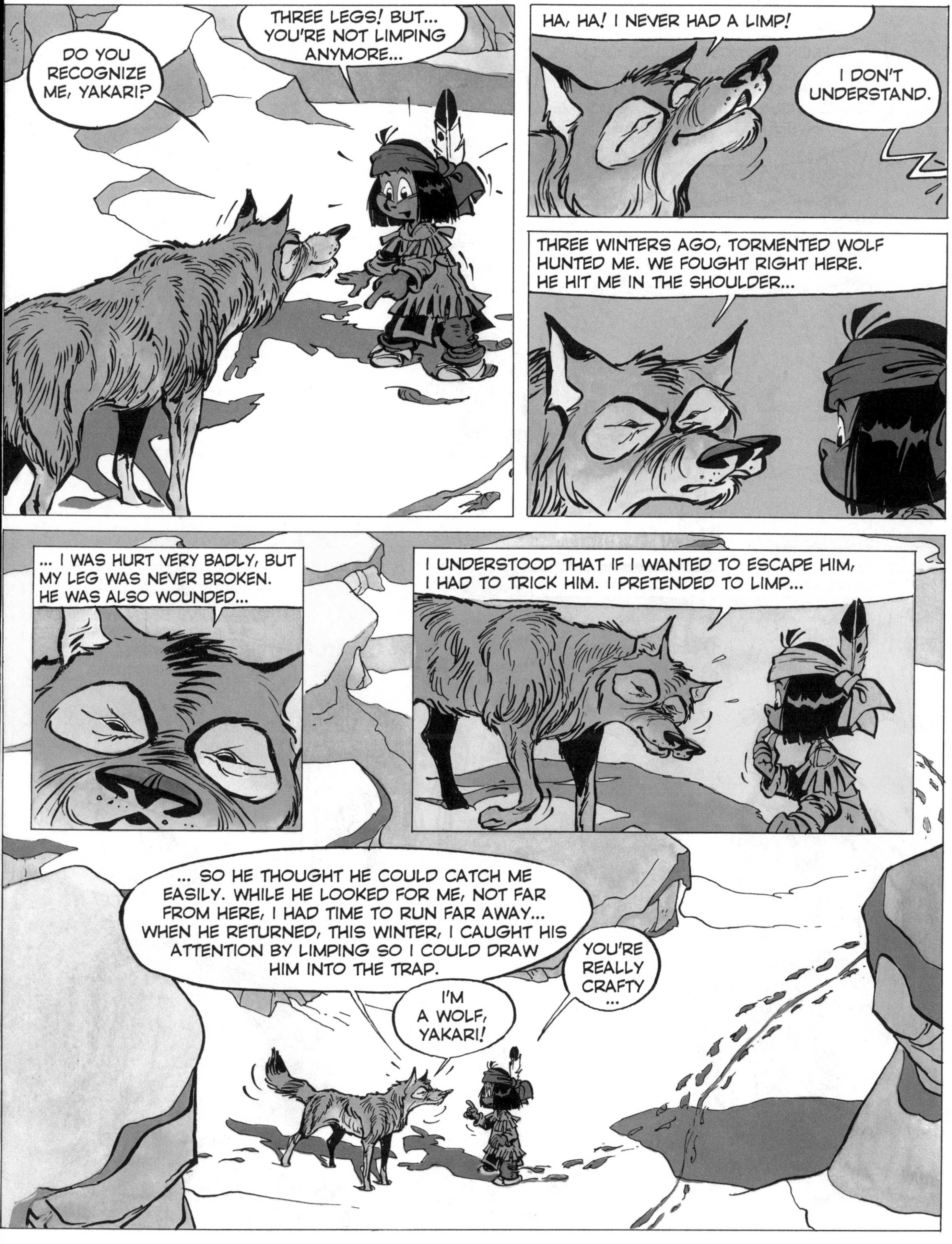
DO YOU RECOGNIZE ME, YAKARI?
THREE LEGS! BUT... YOU'RE NOT LIMPING ANYMORE...
HA, HA! I NEVER HAD A LIMP!
I DON'T UNDERSTAND.
THREE WINTERS AGO, TORMENTED WOLF HUNTED ME. WE FOUGHT RIGHT HERE. HE HIT ME IN THE SHOULDER...
... I WAS HURT VERY BADLY, BUT MY LEG WAS NEVER BROKEN. HE WAS ALSO WOUNDED...
I UNDERSTOOD THAT IF I WANTED TO ESCAPE HIM, I HAD TO TRICK HIM. I PRETENDED TO LIMP...
... SO HE THOUGHT HE COULD CATCH ME EASILY. WHILE HE LOOKED FOR ME, NOT FAR FROM HERE, I HAD TIME TO RUN FAR AWAY... WHEN HE RETURNED, THIS WINTER, I CAUGHT HIS ATTENTION BY LIMPING SO I COULD DRAW HIM INTO THE TRAP.
YOU'RE REALLY CRAFTY ...
I'M A WOLF, YAKARI!

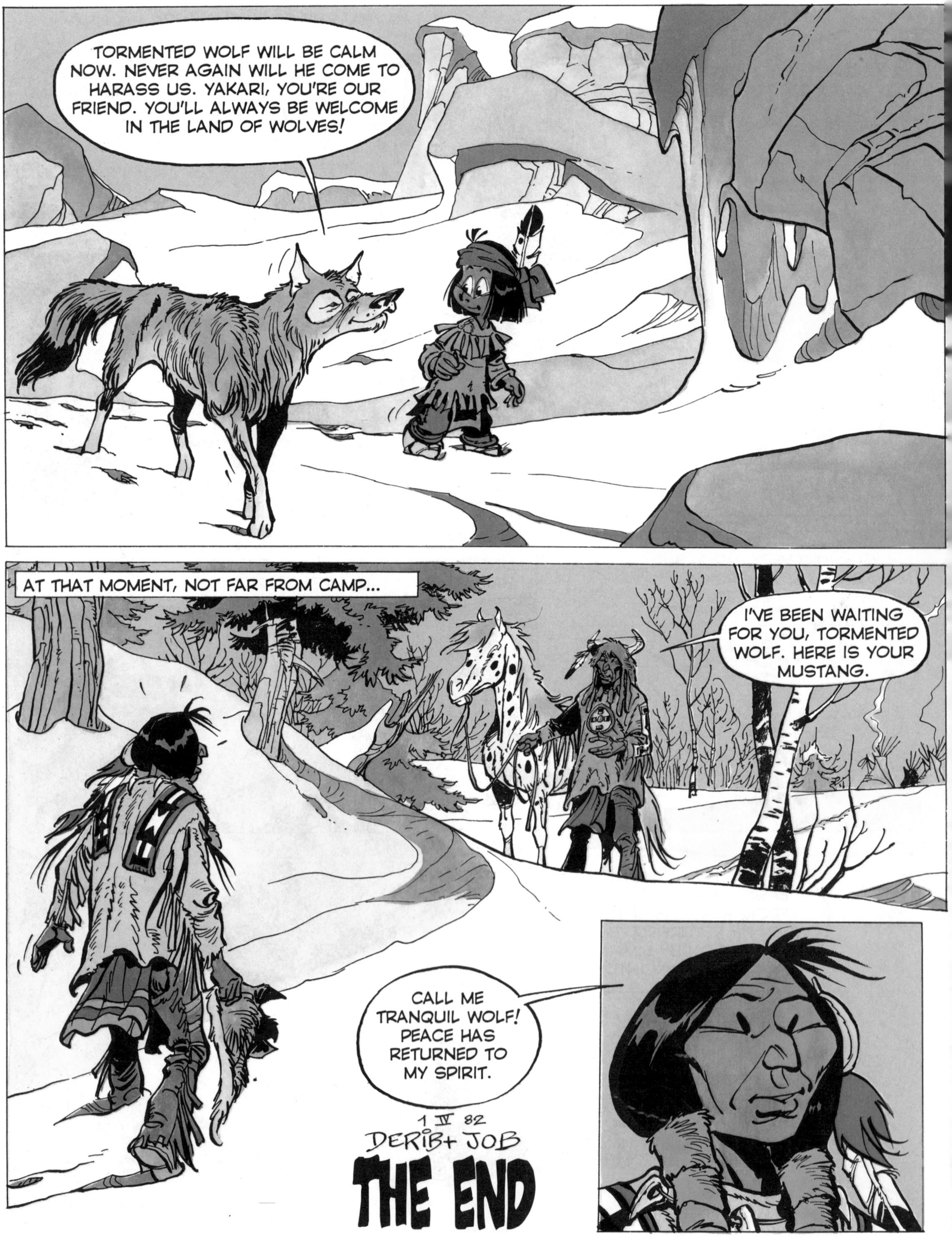
TORMENTED WOLF WILL BE CALM NOW. NEVER AGAIN WILL HE COME TO HARASS US. YAKARI, YOU'RE OUR FRIEND. YOU'LL ALWAYS BE WELCOME IN THE LAND OF WOLVES!
AT THAT MOMENT, NOT FAR FROM CAMP...
I'VE BEEN WAITING FOR YOU, TORMENTED WOLF. HERE IS YOUR MUSTANG.
CALL ME TRANQUIL WOLF! PEACE HAS RETURNED TO MY SPIRIT.
1 IV 82
DERIB+ JOB
THE END